GUN SMOKE

As Parson Price, the man they took for the real Longarm, shook hands with Oregon Bob, Giggles to the left of him and Weedy to the right of him exchanged knowing glances and slapped leather as one.

Price only had time to gasp, "Hold on! You boys have nothing to worry about!" before they both fired, and kept firing, as he melted like candle wax into the sawdust on the floor with one dead hand still firmly grasped by Oregon Bob.

Then another bullet went through Giggles when Willy Cruz fired from the hotel lobby. Another round took Weedy Dorn over the heart while he stood there with an empty six-gun and egg on his face.

But Oregon Bob had yet to draw his Schofield .45 with five in the wheel and he got it out just in time, as Cruz fired through the thick gun smoke at him, only to miss him by a whisker. Then Cruz went down with his smoking gun waving and a .45-28 slug in his own heart, leaving nobody but the barkeep and Oregon Bob on their feet.

The barkeep didn't think it wise to ask a stranger with a smoking Schofield why he'd just taken part in the killings of four other gents. So he dropped limp as a dishrag behind the thick mahogany bar . . .

TABOR EVANS

LONGARM

AND THE LADY HUSTLERS

J

JOVE BOOKS, NEW YORK

This is a work of fiction. Names, characters, places, and incidents either are the product of the author's imagination or are used fictitiously, and any resemblance to actual persons, living or dead, business establishments, events, or locales is entirely coincidental.

LONGARM AND THE LADY HUSTLERS

A Jove Book / published by arrangement with the author

PRINTING HISTORY
Jove edition / March 2003

Copyright © 2003 by Penguin Putnam Inc.

ISBN: 0-515-13493-7

A JOVE BOOK®
Jove Books are published by The Berkley Publishing Group, a division of Penguin Putnam Inc., 375 Hudson Street, New York, New York 10014. JOVE and the "J" design are trademarks belonging to Penguin Putnam Inc.

PRINTED IN THE UNITED STATES OF AMERICA

10 9 8 7 6 5 4 3 2 1

Chapter 1

It was only October. But there was a taste of snow mixed with the smell of cow above the Ogallala stockyards about ten that Saturday morning. So Uncle John Watts and his *segundo*, Willy Cruz, wore wool gloves with their sheepskin jackets as they waited by their hired pens, wishing either for a break in the blue norther or for that son of a bitch buyer to show up before they froze solid.

When Willy Cruz said, "Might that be your Mr. Levine, Uncle John?" his boss regarded the approaching figure uncertainly to declare, "Not unless old Dave's grown some since the last time I druv a herd up this way!"

The approaching figure walked a head taller than most men in a store-bought three-piece suit of tobacco tweed under a black-coffee Stetson, worn Cavalry square, with its crown pancaked Colorado style. Despite a shoestring tie, the stranger strode like a horseman in low-heeled stovepipe boots, and when his frock coat swung open, one could glimpse serious hardware riding cross-draw on his left hip. So Uncle John cautiously decided, "Lawman, if he ain't a hired gun. I ain't at feud with nobody up this way. I did tell you to make sure all our trail herders weren't wanted anywhere's, didn't I?"

Cruz soothed, "Onliest rider we got with papers out on him at all would be young Laredo, and he's only wanted in Mexico, Uncle John."

The older Texan hummed a few bars of that old church hymn called "Farther Along" and, sure enough, before the stranger was near enough to shake, he called out, "Howdy. I'd be Deputy U.S. Marshal Custis Long, and I'm looking for the owner of all these cows, trail-branded Double W, with home brands from all over creation."

Uncle John said, "You found him, Deputy. I'd be John W. Watts, out of Deaf Smith County. This would be my *segundo,* Willy Cruz, and ever' last one of these sixteen hundred head would be mine, all mine, until such time as that infernal Dave Levine turns up to take 'em off our hands!"

The taller and younger man, who'd introduced himself as the lawman better known as Longarm, fished out a three-for-a-nickel cheroot and lit up, bare-handed despite the chill in the air, before he gently but firmly replied, "Only interested in what I'd guesstimate as nine hundred head of black Cherokee beef, Mr. Watts. No offense, but ain't it unusual to round up and trail brand that distinctive breed on the panhandle range of Texas?"

Uncle John nodded easily and explained, "Never got them runty black longhorns in Texas. Added 'em to the stock we started out with as we druv north through the Indian Territory. Got a good price off their Cherokee owners. Figure to net close to five dollars a head up here by the cross-country rails. You want to see our bill of sale? What's all this bullshit about, Deputy Long?"

The tall, tanned man he'd asked smiled thinly, the cheroot gripped at a jaunty angle by his teeth, and replied, "Anybody with pen and paper can whip up a fairly convincing bill of sale. So we're going to have to do better than that, and what this bullshit is about involves some shot-up wards of the federal government and close to a thousand head of black beef critters *they'd* been herding at the time of their demise."

"*Chingate*, we never shot nobody for *las vacas*!" roared Willy Cruz in righteous indignation.

The taller and calmer man in tobacco tweed said, not unkindly, "I never said you did, and if you ever tell me to fuck myself again, I'm likely to cloud up and rain all over you, vaquero!"

"That's enough of that," Uncle John cut in, adding, "We've nothing to hide, Deputy Long. I'm sorry as hell to hear about Mr. Lo, the poor Indian, being robbed by somebody else. But if you'd only be kind enough to read my bills of sale, I'm sure you'll find the names of some *other* fool redskins on 'em!"

The taller man, so addressed, nodded and said, "I'm certain I shall. A man would have to be a total asshole to forge bills of sale with the names of murder victims on 'em. So here's what I aim to do, Mr. Watts. I aim to impound that there herd, all of it, until I can wire the Cherokee Council in Tahlequah for verification of what we have up this way as no more than scribble-scrabble on some paper."

The well-traveled Texican stockman only needed a moment's thought to protest, "Hold on! It's going on Saturday noon, and how can we be sure any government offices, federal or tribal, will still be open by the time you can wire 'em?"

The less worried looking younger man shrugged and easily replied, "We can't. And they'll be shut down all day and tomorrow, seeing it's the Sabbath and all five of the civilized tribes profess Christianity these days. But if you've lawsome title to all that suspicious beef, it won't hurt all that much if you wait 'til Monday to sell it."

"The hell you say!" gasped Uncle John, waving a big-gloved hand at the sea of horns and hide on the far side of the sun-silvered rails as he added, "It's costing us two

3

bits a head every day we board all this beef in these here fucking yards! They got to be fed. They got to be watered, thrice a fucking day, and the buyer I've cut a deal with will be here any minute to take the load off my poor old shoulders! I ain't paid up past noon and . . . Jesus H. Christ, even if my buyer don't go somewheres else, I'll wind up out of pocket by . . . let's see, now . . ."

"Four hundred dollars a day," observed his tormentor, cheerfully, before deciding, "Eight hundred if you don't sell off before Monday noon. But you just now said you had a buyer, right?"

"You can't do this to me!" wailed the older Texan as he considered the edge Buyer Levine was going to have, come Monday, once he learned the Double W beef had to be sold off *fast*!

The younger and taller man in tobacco tweed just stood there with his cheroot gripped jaunty in his sort-of-wolfish smile.

Uncle John hesitated, then lowered his voice to implore, "What if I was to, ah, post a bond with you, personal, Deputy Long?"

The man holding things up in low-heeled army boots asked in as quiet a tone, "You mean you'd be offering to deposit say a dollar a head with me until such time as the Cherokee Nation can verify your right to sell the herd, come Monday?"

Uncle John said, "Not exactly, and that's a hell of a lot of *dinero* you're demanding, even if you let me sell this morning, if you see what I mean!"

The younger man in control of the action shrugged and replied in an easy tone, "Sixteen hundred dollars ain't about to pay for the egg on my face if you gents are pulling a fast one on this child! What if I get a wire from Tahlequah saying I'm supposed to arrest you and you've sold their stolen beef and skipped town?"

"You'll have sixteen hundred dollars of mine to keep

4

and cherish," soothed the older man, who sighed and added, "Ain't no way we can reclaim our bond from anybody if we ain't here, is there?"

He saw the younger man seemed hesitant and insisted, "I got it in gold certificates here in my money belt. Do we have us a deal?"

"I'd say it sounds suspiciously like the offer of a bribe!" replied the now sort-of-edgy younger man, who went on to explain, "If it was to get out that I'd let a stolen herd be sold and shipped right out from under me, I'd never in this world explain sixteen hundred in pocket money without blushing!"

Uncle John smiled dirty and suggested, "In that case, it might be best to just keep the money our own little secret. But don't worry about such a disaster, Deputy Long. I ain't about to leave town before you get your wire and I get my bond back. So how's about it?"

They had to argue a mite more. But, in the end, Uncle John was free to sell his beef that morning, with a receipt for his sixteen-hundred-dollar federal bond in another pocket of his sheepskins to go with as clear a conscience as he'd been professing.

The man he'd paid off left the stockyards to move against a pungent prevailing wind toward his hotel near the Union Pacific depot. Having a room key in his pocket, he strode through the shady lobby and up the stairs to let himself into Room 2-F without knocking.

He'd told the bodacious bleached blonde reclining on the bed to shoot through the door at any cocksucker who knocked, and she looked capable of doing so.

Her current name was Zilphia La Belle, and she'd never again see thirty, nor less than a hundred and forty pounds. But she still knew how to use what she had to work with and, better yet, how to lay low and keep her mouth shut when a gentleman of the road was out fleecing marks.

As he shut the door behind him and peeled off his hat,

coat and six-gun, Zilphia dimpled up at him to ask, "So how did it go, my beamish boy with the fake moustache?"

Parson Price, as he was better known in his own circle, peeled off the heroic handlebars and, at the same time, got rid of the cheroot he detested, confiding, "Like clockwork. I figure on another score this afternoon, once the Double W crew vacates the stockyards to await my returning their bond at their own hotel down the way. I asked around the yards earlier, and now I've got my sights on another panhandle herd out of Castro County. But I'm all yours to cuddle and spoon until, say, half past two."

The big, brassy blonde rolled on her back to let her kimono fall open as she spread the red garters of her black mesh stocking with an uncertain chuckle, asking, "Shouldn't we quit while we're ahead, dear little piggy? What if any of the marks you've taken get together to compare notes before we've hit the road? What if that lawman you've been pretending to be hits town before we can get out of it?"

"You worry too much about my foolproof stings," soothed the con man as he shucked his shirt and sat on the bed beside her. He peeled off his new boots and pants, explaining, "Nobody who's posted bond with a well-known federal lawman is going to even suspect they might not get their money back until the famous Longarm, not I, fails to show up in the cold gray dawn. By which time we'll be many a railroad stop away, in any direction."

Rolling nude to join Zilphia atop the bedding in the right romantic broad daylight, Parson Price took her in his arms to continue, "And since I won't be in town to question, who can question the right of a famous federal lawman to question the ownership of possibly purloined property herded across more than one state line?"

As Parson Price proceeded to run his free palm down across the Junoesque ups and down of her soft smooth body, Zilphia pointed out, "There's *one* party who's apt to question the piss out of you if he discovers you've been shaking stockmen down in his name, and I'm scared, honey lamb. I've heard the real Longarm is awesomely sharp as well as dangerous to mess with!"

Wetting two fingers inside her, before he began to pet her turgid clit for her, Parson Price easily replied, "Who's messing with anybody but you, sweet momma? Credit this child with at least a little common sense. Like I told you, coming in aboard the U.P., I'd read that issue of the *Rocky Mountain News*. The real Longarm has been bearing witness at the trial of some train robbers he arrested last summer."

His well-padded bed partner murmured, "Not so rough. Just glide your wet fingers softly over the strings of my old banjo and . . . Yes, that feels nice. How come you had to pretend to be a real lawman in the first place? Wouldn't it have been safer to just say you were some made-up deputy marshal, dear?"

Parson Price kissed his way up her throat to nibble her ear before he explained, "Neither safer nor half as foolproof, doll. There's only so many federal lawman, anywhere. Old boys are always getting themseves exposed, at mighty awkward times, by pretending to be army officers or government officials who can't be dug out of the files most every newspaper and town marshal ought to keep. I remember this poor old bird who'd almost scored big as an Indian agent with fat government agency contracts to be distributed amongst his favorite pals."

As he rolled between her lush thighs to settle his naked lap into hers, he said, "The cattle barons he'd accepted all those bribes from were not content to just tar and feather the man once they had most of their money back. They tarred him. They feathered him. Then they left him gut-shot on a prairie ant pile."

As he began to move in her, and vice versa, Parson

7

Price insisted, "He'd have got away with it, but it only took one suspicious wire to Washington to expose the sad story of a less clever fibber than me."

She said, "Let me get on top if you don't want to *move* your sweet ass, you big fibber."

But he assured her he liked things just the way they were, and then he proved it by moving in and out of her fast enough to make her forget further thoughts about the real Longarm.

But this was not to say that nobody at all was worried about the real Longarm in Ogallala as, somewhere in the distance, a clock struck noon.

In another, darker, hotel room, the pard who'd been out scouting was a female member of the team and she knocked, sneaky, to be let in by another underling, at gunpoint.

Their leader, Lefty Lindwood, was seated astride a bentwood chair near the jalousied window, calm as a sidewinder fixing to strike, as he demanded, "Well, did you get a close look at him or, better yet, find out where he's staying, here in Ogallala?"

The nondescript sparrow, who was only sort-of-pretty when one looked at her twice, said, "I was able to look him over, tight, as he strutted both ways with that double-action .44-40 you told me to watch for. I was close enough to overhear him introduce himself as Longarm at the stockyards, and I followed him back to his hotel, down the way, which happens to be the Ogallala Overland Rest and he's in room 2-F."

The middle-aged southpaw, wearing a .38 Colt Lightning on his left hip, side draw, muttered, "That tears it. Longarm knows me on sight and the son of a bitch is farsighted. I don't see how a man is supposed to rob a bank holed up in this hotel room. So we're going to have to kill the bastard afore he finds out I'm here in Ogallala!"

A younger member of the small but deadly gang quietly asked, "Do I hear any volunteers? They say Longarm's sort of dangerous, boss!"

To which Lefty Lindwood replied in a nasty purr, "He ain't *sort* of dangerous. He's *damned* dangerous! So here's how we'd better kill him."

Chapter 2

Seeing he had the full attention of the two women and three other men in the small, dark room, Lefty Lindwood said, "Ain't nobody draws faster nor shoots straighter than the one and original Custis Long and, after that, he seems to have eyes in the back of his head. More than one sincere attempt to backshoot the big bastard has ended in disaster for our kind. So let us consider his possible weak spots, instead of his strong points."

The less mousy gal in the gang, the auburn-haired Verona O'Shay, absently smoothed her forest-green velvet riding habit to say, "I've yet to meet the famous Longarm, but I've heard he has an eye for the ladies."

Lefty passed on the cheap shot about ladies, albeit that wasn't easy, and shook his head. "I fear he has all his bad habits on a tighter rein than most. He drinks, but holds his liquor well. If he can't smoke on a stakeout, he just kicks the habit for as long as it may require. He's good at poker and likes to play, but, as in the case of his smoking and drinking, he knows when to fold and walk away when the game's getting in the way of his more serious desires."

"What might he find more serious than smoking or

drinking or playing cards?" asked the mousy-but-sort-of-pretty Phoebe Blake, a vision of indistinction in her slate gray topcoat and fuzzy black head scarf.

The more spectacular Verona smiled and said, "I just told all of us, Phoebe. He likes girls. A lot."

Lefty Lindwood shook his cadaverous skull and insisted, "Not to the point of easy assassination. Some blame it on his romantic nature, whilst others figure he has some sixth sense about womankind. But in either case, Longarm don't pay for his slap and tickle and even when it's offered free he seems to sidestep woman trouble the way a housefly escapes the swatter without appearing to study on it. So the old border game of luring a sucker up a dark alley with a raised hem don't work on him worth spit. He circled the block to get the drop on the last bunch who tried that. Catching folk like us seems his greatest desire."

"All right, he can't be beat to the draw, backshot or lured into a trap. So what's left?" asked Giggles Gleason, the ever-smiling youngest male in the bunch.

Lefty said, "Unexpected treachery. On the part of a fellow lawman he trusts. Allowing for some Wild West bullshit in the papers, he's come close as hell to dying at the hands of crooked fellow lawmen. He's on record as having said it was a good thing he'd commenced to suspect such pals just before it came time to slap leather. So what if Longarm was to meet up with a fellow lawman he had no reason at all to suspect? Say a bounty hunter after the same wild bunch?"

Little Phoebe demurely inquired, "Where are we going to recruit such a trustworthy sneak and what wild bunch might they both be after?"

Lefty laughed and said, "Hell, girl, *we* have to be the bunch Longarm is after, here in Ogallala. Why else would he be here? Some two-faced cuss I'm still working on must have tipped the Justice Department that yours truly has recruited a new gang after getting out of Leavenworth early with the help of that greased federal judge. Longarm was one of the lawmen who arrested this child, going on six years ago. They know he'd know me on sight from across the street in tricky light. That has to be the reason they have him, instead of the Nebraska marshals, after us, this far from Longarm's Denver District Court."

Nobody there argued with that logic. So Lefty Lindwood went on to say, "It would be suicide for *me* to move in on Longarm with him on the prod for me, personal. But have any of you three boys ever laid eyes on the son of a bitch, or vice versa?"

Giggles giggled and said, "Phoebe, here, is the only one of us who's seen him up close, here in Ogallala, boss."

Lefty said, "I noticed. That's my point. I got the badges you boys can use among the other souvenirs in my saddlebags. I got an onionskin of the all-points warning out on us, down Kansas way, too. So what say some green but otherwise innocent looking youths wearing badges were to call on Longarm at his hotel, or better yet, the hotel taproom in the tricky light of the supper hour to wave them papers out on us and ask the advice of an older and wiser man hunter?"

Giggles giggled, "Hot damn! I see it now! As he's reading all them bad things about us, we all three slap leather at once, right?"

Lefty said, "Wrong. He's been known to palm a double derringer for a spell as he gets to know strangers amid strange surroundings. You let him read the all-points. You let it sink in that the four of you are on the same side. Then you get him to pontificate on how such *travieso* bastards might be located in these parts. You get him to feeling good about you and then somewhere along the line where it won't seem the least bit suspicious, whichever one of you who gets the chance laughs and puts out a hand to shake on sharing the credit for arresting me yet again."

He let that sink in and added, "Then, with one of you holding on to his gun hand for dear life, if you know what's good for all three of you, the other two draw and empty their wheels into the bastard, point-blank, before all three of you light out, with the one who shook hands covering the retreat with his own loaded six-gun, see?"

They did. Giggles giggled and little Phoebe said, "Ooh, you're so clever, and so mean, Lefty!"

The older and more serious Weedy Dorn exchanged poker-faced nods with the red-haired Oregon Bob Cooke as Verona O'Shay decided, "Phoebe is right, Lefty. You're mean and sneaky as a wolverine, but smart as a fox while you're about it. But I've still got a question. How do you boys mean to move in on that bank like innocent cattle drovers after gunning a federal lawman in public in a town this size?"

Lefty said, "The uncertain light of evening was chosen with that in mind and, of course, the boys will change outfits and we'll all hold off a few days after the killing. The idea is to get Longarm off the streets of Ogallala so they'll be safer for *us*, see? Nobody else here in town has any reason to suspect toad squat about any one of us. Comes time the big bastard's dead body cools down, the newspapers will have figured his killing as some owlhoot rider's revenge. Lord knows Longarm has plenty of other enemies to spare."

He rose to move over to the saddle draped across the foot rail of his hired bed as he went on, "The law in these parts will be on the prod for gunslicks slapping leather on lawmen. Where in my simple plan does it say anything about guarding the damned bank?"

His simple question inspired hysterical giggles from Giggles Gleason and amused laughter from everyone else as Lefty rummaged in his saddlebag for those badges and the all-points onionskin.

As he handed them out, Lefty warned, "The outfits you boys have on were chose to make you seem trail hands, and you'll want to wear them to that bank job when things cool down. So, I want you to go out this afternoon and buy yourselves some store-bought woolen suits like lawmen in town would be more apt to wear. Pick up some derby hats to wear instead of them three Stetsons. Even in good light, a head under a new derby looks different than the same head under a trail-worn Stetson. Your gun rigs, worn under your fancy new frock coats, won't be recalled in detail and this is no time to break in new gun rigs!"

There came a murmur of agreement. As Giggles got to the door first, Lefty Lindwood said, "I want you watching Longarm's hotel this afternoon, Phoebe. Verona, I'd as soon you stayed here with this child for now, savvy?"

Verona savvied. So she grinned like a mean little kid. Phoebe savvied as well. So she was cheerful as a wet hen when she left the two of them alone for some high noon fornication.

It was *cold* outside and before that shanty Irish cunt had horned in, little Phoebe had been the one the cadaverous but well-endowed and right imaginative older man had been screwing regular, with imagination.

Moving down the hotel stairs with her lips pursed tight, Phoebe told herself not to picture Lefty and Verona going sixty-nine like that, God damn their naked hides, but of course she did, and consoled herself with the hope Lefty might wind up hurting the bigger but smaller-built Verona when, not if, he decided he fancied some Greek-style slap and tickle.

Out on the streets of Ogallala, the wind had died some and the sun shone down a tad warmer, but Phoebe could still make out her own breath as she trudged south toward the Ogallala Overland Rest. There was a Mex chili parlor across from that hotel's front entrance. Phoebe decided to stake out yonder, at a window table, where a body could get warmer inside and out whilst she waited to see what Longarm might be up to next.

Phoebe ordered sunnyside-up eggs over her chili con carne with plenty of sugar and cream in her coffee. The hardwood chair under her had a raised rim to its seat and once a wet hen moved her bottom about, just right, it was possible to relieve an engorged clit a mite by sort of rocking back and forth on the edge whilst she went through the motions with her chili con carne.

That Denver girl she'd spent a night locked up with, down K.C. way, had most likely just been making up that dirty story about the time the man called Longarm had shacked up with her and two other whores down on Larimer Steet. But she'd sure made the adventure sound interesting. And now the boys were fixing to murder Longarm before she'd ever get the chance to find out whether any man could really make a lady come eight times in one night. Phoebe found herself idly wondering whether scouting such an enemy up close and more personal would be considered treason to her own side. Lefty had *said* to find out as much as she could about the goings and comings of Deputy U.S. Marshal Custis Long, and how could her coming along with his comings hurt and . . . Dear Jesus, those Mexicans in the back were staring at her curious, and she just couldn't stop herself from pleasuring her lonesome crotch no matter what they thought!

Then Phoebe Blake abandoned her love seat and half-eaten snack she'd paid ahead for. She sprang up to head outside as, from behind, one of the waitresses murmured something in Spanish.

To which a more Americanized fellow waitress replied,

"Do not hope to dream such things. The fantasy is *never* better than a real fuck!"

Phoebe had dashed out into the cold with all her appetites less than satisfied because Longarm, or the man they thought was Longarm, had just emerged from the hotel to head toward the railroad depot, walking fast in those army boots on his far longer legs.

Keeping to the shaded walk on her side, Phoebe trailed her quarry catty-corner, with the dust of noonday hooves and wagon wheels hanging in the crisp sunshine between them. As she did so, she wondered where he was headed now, and how come he was dressed so lightly in spite of the blue norther nobody else seemed to be enjoying.

They called such cold dry spells blue northers on the Great Plains because, at such times, the arctic winds coming down out of the north blew dry under a sunny sky of indigo blue, with nary a cloud to be seen. Blue northers usually ended with a more dangerous, but somewhat warmer, blizzard when a less usual Chinook out of the west raised the temperature twenty or more degrees within as many minutes.

Thanks to the cold snap, only those with serious business were out on the streets of Ogallala that noon and Phoebe found it duck-soup simple to trail the tall figure in distinctive tobacco tweed at a good safe distance. She decided he had to be wearing two union suits of red flannel under his thin frock coat, albeit he still cut a tall, slender figure that made a gal who hadn't been getting any want to strum her own banjo. Then she saw where he was headed and forgot about her less important worries. The tall, tanned rascal was entering the bank Lefty and the boys were planning to rob the moment the coast seemed clear!

Hoping Longarm might be cashing a check, exchanging specie for paper or vice versa, Phoebe waited until he was inside a spell before she broke cover to cross over and

17

pussyfoot in after him, taking a twenty-dollar silver certificate from her muff-purse to explain what she'd come in for, herself.

But the bank was crowded inside, seeing it was fixing to close early of a Saturday, and Phoebe never had to break her bill as she stood in line just long enough to make certain the man she'd followed inside was not in any of the other lines. He had to be in the *back*, discussing more serious matters with one of the bank officials!

Phoebe left the bank like a crawfishing shadow to leg it back to their hotel and drift like smoke up the back stairs. As she came to the door Lefty and Verona had shut and bolted for some sincere privacy, Phoebe heard the bigger gal who'd replaced her in Lefty's bed pleading with Lefty not to shove that big mean thing in *there*, for heaven's sake.

Phoebe smiled dirty, recalling how Lefty had confided all longtime convicts got sort of used to coming that way. She raised a small gloved fist to knock, a certain way.

On the far side, Lefty Lindwood protested, "Aw, shit, this had better be important!"

Phoebe said, "It is."

When Lefty opened up, stark naked but gun in hand, to let her in, he demanded, "What the fuck are you doing here? I told you to follow Longarm this afternoon, girl!"

Ignoring the auburn-haired nude atop the bed covers— auburn-haired all over—the petite brunette replied, "I did. I followed him into Stockman's Savings and Loans. He's in the back with the management, even as we speak. You were right about him *knowing*, Lefty! Somebody tipped the law off about your plans for Stockman's Savings and Loans! So you and the boys will be walking into a stakeout if you hit that bank."

Lefty threw the brass bolt behind her as he nodded soberly and told her, "You just saved our asses, Phoebe girl. But there's more than one bank in town and whilst

Longarm may know this child is in Ogallala, he would have shown up here by now if he had the least notion *where* I was in town. So once we put him in his grave, we'll be free to rob *another* bank as fat and sassy with money from all these fall sales."

Moving back to the bed to reholster his Lightning and set his bare ass down some more, Lefty patted the covers between him and Verona as he added with a sort of dirty smile, "Seeing I now have a whole lot of new plans to make, why don't you strip off all that itchy wool and join us in some . . . contemplating, Phoebe girl?"

To which the little sparrow could only chirp, with a radiant smile, "I was afraid you were never going to ask!"

Chapter 3

About two hundred miles to the west-southwest, under the same crisp, cloudless sky, the District Court of Denver was knocking off early for Saturday afternoon because the fair but firm Judge Dickerson felt a wry pity for the just convicted and didn't want to leave them in suspense over the Sabbath about his fair but firm sentence.

When a defense lawyer objected that the punishment hardly seemed to fit the crime, Judge Dickerson just smiled and said, "I am not hanging your clients for robbing trains, Counselor. I am hanging all but the baby of the bunch lest more trains be robbed out our way. You'll admit, I feel certain, that once a gang's robbed one train, more trains are sure to be robbed if they ever get loose. And we all know how short a human life must seem to the sons of bitches who keep turning lifers loose on us less than ten years down the damned road!"

Nodding at the convicted train robbers, not unkindly, the silver-haired federal judge repeated, "Life at hard labor for Sonny Carver, there, and death by hanging for Weaver, Brown and Robinson."

As lesser lawmen moved in to drag the prisoners out, Judge Dickerson pounded his gavel and yelled, "Court's adjourned. But I want Deputy Long to join me in my chambers, now."

So the real Longarm, who fit the description but didn't look that much like the smooth-shaven Parson Price pretending to be him over in Ogallala, followed the older man back to the oak-paneled inner chambers of the federal courthouse, hoping this wasn't about Miss Bubbles from the stenography pool down the hall.

If he'd warned the pneumatic blonde once, he'd warned her a dozen times, about screwing on that leather chesterfield in the judge's chambers.

But as they entered the judge's chambers that afternoon, with the older man looking way too sore to ask whether Miss Bubbles put out as often as some said, Judge Dickerson said, "Shut the door. This is an off-the-record private grudge. Do you recall that bank-robbing Kansas rider, Jethro or Lefty Lindwood, I sentenced to life at hard labor after you made the mistake of bringing him back alive?"

Longarm had to think. He'd brought down the hall as many as he could in the six or eight years he'd been riding for Marshal Billy Vail. Then the penny dropped and Longarm said, "Lean, mean balding cuss? Looked like a lunger but healthy enough to ride all day and screw all night?"

Judge Dickerson moved around to his side of the desk and waved Longarm to a guest seat that matched the chesterfield Miss Bubbles like to screw on. "That's him. It was my fond wish he spend the rest of his life in the Jefferson Barracks, over to Leavenworth. But they let him out early on good behavior. That's what they call it when a man locked up in a federal prisons fails to commit murder, rape or arson for a spell. Good behavior."

Longarm resisted the desire for a smoke as he leaned back in the padded cordovan leather to soberly reply, "You just explained, out front, why you thought it better

22

to hang habitual criminals, Your Honor. May one hope Lefty Lindwood has done something habitual enough to be arrested since he graduated early?"

Judge Dickerson bitched, "He's dropped out of sight. Total. But you know what they say about a leopard changing his spots. And by a curious coincidence five known associates of Lindwood have vanished from human ken as well!"

Rummaging among the papers on his desk, Judge Dickerson produced a typed-up list to read off, "Full-time thief and occasional bank robber called Weedy Dorn. Oregon Bob Cooke and a new addition they describe as Giggles Gleason. Oregon Bob is the one who's done time with Lindwood. Weedy and Giggles are suspected of stopping a stage in Oregon Bob's distinguished company, shortly before his pal, Lefty Lindwood, got out in some manner I'd like to know more about.

"The gang left Kansas just days ago for parts unknown, along with a couple of doxies said to be more dangerous than your average slut. Bitty brunette and a bigger Irish-looking gal with uncertain names they keep changing to fit the occasion. The little one's said to have disolved an unhappy marriage with a .32 Harrington Richardson under the name of Widow Thornhill née Blake. Her auburn-haired pal carved up another whore in Dodge with a busted bottle before getting out of town leaving neither a forwarding address nor a certain name. She seems to fancy the letter *V* as in *virgin*. Likes to be called Victoria, Valhalla, Verona and such. How do you like it so far?"

To which Longarm could only reply, "Not that much, no offense, Your Honor. Old Lefty and his new pals sound colorful enough to appear in Ned Buntline's *Wild West* magazine. But what have they *done*? What, if any, federal charge might we have on even one of 'em?"

Judge Dickerson shrugged and said, "Have a little patience. They only let Lefty out a few weeks ago. He suffers delusions of intelligence and likes to plan ahead before he pulls a no-smarter-than-average robbery. If they follow his usual method, they'll drift casual into town to set up quarters near the bank and wait 'til nobody seems to recall them as all that new in town."

Longarm nodded thoughtfully and declared, "That was the mistake the James-Younger gang made over in Northfield back in '76. Rode into town wearing matched dusters to cover their trail clothes and had the locals wondering about 'em before they made it to the bank. Familiar, albeit unknown, faces ought to find it easier to move in around closing time and then what? They hole up in their nearby hired quarters whilst the townees posse up and ride out in ever' direction, scouting for sign?"

Judge Dickerson grimaced and replied, "That was the stunt Lindwood was trying when you caught him at it half a dozen years ago. Of course, he's had lots of time to consider the errors of his earlier ways. Lord knows exactly what they're planning right now. But knowing the ways of spotted leopards it's a safe bet they're planning *something*, somewhere."

Longarm usually got his orders from Billy Vail down the hall. But since the marshal backing the Denver District Court took *his* orders off the same, Longarm simply nodded and asked, "What might the court direct us to do about your missing suspects with no wants or warrants out on them, Your Honor?"

Judge Dickerson frowned and said, "Don't get fresh with me, young sir. It would be nice if you could find out where Lefty and his gang might be, planning what. But I agree it's a big country and you're not paid to be sent on a fool's errands to El Dorado or the Big Rock Candy Mountains. So we'll use the excuse of suspecting Lefty Lindwood's up to something to have you sniff around his last known address in Leavenworth, see?"

Longarm blinked and confessed, "Not hardly, Your

Honor. Didn't you just now tell me Lefty and his gang ain't *around* Leavenworth no more?"

"The corrupt sons of bitches who prostituted their law degrees to cut him loose are still in Kansas, and Lefty Lindwood wasn't the first and may not be the last lifer to be somehow shoehorned out of that federal prison. I want to know who the *fixer* is. I want to know real bad!"

Longarm asked, "Wouldn't the names of the legal eagles who filed such appeal be on record, Your Honor? And wouldn't the names of the judges who approved early releases be on file as well?"

The sterner senior judge snapped, "I'm not after legal hacks. They've yet to build enough jails to hold half the courthouse gangs in our land of opportunity. I said I wanted the name of the *fixer*. The Mr. Big, the wise money crook who pays off to apply the right political pressures to the pathetic hacks we elect to run this country."

He let that sink in before he explained, "We're sending you in undercover, arriving under an assumed name we'll assume we have some serious federal charges on. I won't waste time instructing you on the ways one strikes up conversations in saloons frequented by riders of the owl-hoot trail. Feel free to gamble and whore more than President Hayes and Miss Lemonade Lucy might approve, as long as you're not actually committing any federal offenses. Let it get around you're a rather sinister young man with no visible means of support but money to spend if anyone there knows how to keep you out of jail. We'll work from this end to let it be known you're wanted on charges you're just too shy to talk about and, hell, what else do you need, a diagram on the damned chalk board?"

Longarm said, "I know how to work undercover, Your Honor, and I have to allow your devious plan sounds like more fun than usual. I'll tell my boss, Marshal Vail, and

I'm sure he'll have our clerk-typist draw up my travel orders over the weekend."

Judge Dickerson said, "Marshal Vail and young Henry will have left the building by now. I gave the orders to Billy this morning. There'll be no travel orders cut by anybody. Officially, we're not sending you anywhere. You'll be carried on the books as a peace officer on leave. There'll be no need to record where you went for your well-earned rest.

"We'll be filing no records because we just won't know, officially, how some practical joker with a sick sense of humor put out some forged arrest warrants on some saddle tramp this court has never heard of. How do you like *them* apples, Deputy Long?"

Longarm smiled thinly and replied, "I can see how your ass might be covered, no offense, Your Honor. But what about this child, raising ned in Kansas under an assumed name as he scouts up a good lawyer?"

Judge Dickerson explained, "Nobody by any name we decide on will be tried in any court on any warrant issued by some unknown practical joker. But since there's no way for the victim of such a cruel hoax to know he doesn't really need a good lawyer, by which we mean a very bad *man*. It'll all blow over, after you've gotten the names of said good lawyers and the fixer they'll turn in if they ever mean to practice law in any federal court in this land again!"

Longarm shrugged and decided, "Ours not to reason why and like I said, it sounds like a nice change of pace. I won't have to wear this infernal suit and tie as I head east to Leavenworth, right?"

Judge Dickerson said, "That's for certain. But you're not to show up in those faded denims you favor for field missions, either. I want you to appear more tinhorn. Like a man who has plenty of money as well as no taste in brocaded vests and say a silk cravat with a fake diamond stick pin to go with that white, ten-gallon hat."

Longarm protested, "I'd as soon wear one of them Spanish hats with as flat a crown as this one, Your Honor. I'm used to moving through tight spaces in duds of current dimensions."

Judge Dickerson smiled wickedly, which was not a pretty sight, and decided Longarm could pick his new duds and charge 'em to His Honor's personal account as long as everything looked tinhorn. He said, "I don't think I'll let you see the fake warrants fitting your flashy new description. That way, you'll sound like an experienced liar when you deny knowing anything about any lousy warrants."

Longarm shook his head and protested, "I'm already an experienced liar and that's a damn fool notion, no offense, Your Honor."

As the older man glared, Longarm explained, "You show me an owlhoot rider who really can't say what he's wanted for, and I'll show you some other cuss pretending to be him. You mind that punk down Tombstone way who got the shit kicked out of him when he bragged on being the one and original Billy the Kid? Some old boys who'd read the murder warrant out on William H. Bonney found the imposter's tale unconvincing when he was unable to name the sheriff he was accused of murdering. I mean to know exactly what I'm supposed to be wanted for as I sincerely deny knowing anyone is after me at all, see?"

The judge did. He was no fool. He nodded and told Longarm to get to work on his new appearance and identity, adding, "If you leave Denver on the Sunday night train, you'll have all Monday to settle in before you commence to hit the saloons of Leavenworth. Report to me at my own home, about this time tomorrow, so I can look you over while we decide on a name to issue those warrants on. You'll want to be off the train in Kansas before our practical joker wires Leavenworth. It would never do to have you walk into a stakeout in the depot. We want to give you time to sort of fit in before it gets around that you're wanted on a serious federal charge, see?"

Longarm said, "I got a slicker notion, Your Honor. What if I show up under one name, with that warrant out on a man by another name, who fits the same description and seems inclined to whistle 'Aura Lee' whenever he's fixing to call, playing five-card stud?"

" 'Aura Lee'?" Judge Dickerson frowned.

Longarm hummed a few bars and tossed in, " 'The angels came down, in the night, and stole my Aura Lee,' Your Honor. The pathetical sweet song was popular with both sides during the war, but it ain't heard all that often, lately."

The judge chuckled and said, "I follow your drift. We let them think they're smart as they figure out who you really might be. You hint at your need for a slick lawyer, without saying why you need a lawyer. Have you ever thought of selling gold bricks for a living, Deputy Long?"

Longarm shrugged and said, "Folk are always most willing to believe lies they tell themselves. Ask any back-fence gossip if it ain't a lot more convincing to count off the months since a wedding than it is to hear the bride confess she wasn't really entitled to wear white. Just charge this child with something under one name and I'll see everyone figures I'm fibbing when I introduce myself in Kansas under another!"

So they shook on it, and Longarm legged it down to Larimer Street to charge some cheap flash to His Honor's expense account. Stores of course stayed open to catch fresh-paid shoppers leaving early on a crisp Saturday afternoon. Shopping for a tinhorn, he decided to call himself Frank Mason, because it sounded so phoney, it was fun. Longarm sprang for a going-on-lavender frock coat over a brocaded, mostly burnt-orange, vest to clash with a sort-of-deep-purple Spanish hat. They sold heaps of vaudeville costumery along Larimer Street.

He naturally left his more serious and well-broken-in army boots and cross-draw gun rig, as they fit with his new outfit. But the results were comical and Longarm was sort of looking forward to frightening horses on the streets of Leavenworth by the time he was ready to leave for there the next evening.

But he never left for Leavenworth because, like that great sage had warned, it's a tangled web we weave when first we practice to deceive, and the best laid plans of mice and men can go to hell in a hack.

Chapter 4

Like many a follower of crooked logic, Phoebe Blake had been too clever by half in mistaking Parson Price's visit to Stockman's Savings and Loans for what it hadn't been. The con man shaking stockmen down by pretending to be Longarm had simply dropped by the nearest good-sized bank in town to exchange currency, and they'd naturally told him he'd have to talk to one of the boys in the backroom about that kind of cash.

Herd drivers and buyers perforce having to deal in heaps of money had to pack it in the form of paper and fresh-printed U.S. Treasury notes as crinkled just-so were trustworthy enough in broad day when you were used to snapping the same, one right after the other. But barkeeps, hotel clerks or other smaller businessmen were still inclined to demand hard currency, because it was so much tougher to fake real gold or silver.

So a traveling man, with heaps of travel and no strong impressions in his wake in mind, wanted at least ten pounds or so of money-belt double eagles under his frock coat when he turned back into a man of the cloth accompanied by a pleasantly plump *niece* few people in Ogallala were likely to recall, thanks to the wonders of room service and the ways a woman could change her appearance without half trying.

Phoebe hadn't been watching when Price carried the sack of specie back to their hotel to load up his money belt and leave it in the safe care of Miss Zilphia La Belle before he sallied forth to see how much more paper money they'd be leaving town with, come Sunday evening.

The innocent-looking sparrow Lefty Lindwood had tailing him was experimenting with the customs of the Isle of Lesbos at one end and old-fashioned Greek at the other when Parson Price, as Deputy U.S. Marshal Custis Long, was shaking down, or demanding, another cattle baron post bond on his own twelve-hundred head until such time as Longarm would be able to verify he'd come by them honest, in spite of those Mexican home brands you didn't usually see on properly brung-up Texas beef.

There came an awkward moment, heading back to his hotel with an even wad of treasury notes, when Parson Price met up with the *segundo* of the Double W he'd visited with that morning. Willy Cruz was leaning against the rails near the corner of the stockyards, jawing with another breed-dressed cow, and whilst he howdied "Long-arm" friendly enough, he still asked how come the taller man was still loitering around out that way, seeing Willy thought they had a deal.

Parson Price replied in a jovial tone, "I was fixing to ask you the same question, you suspicious looking Texican. Like I told you and your boss, earlier, I've been inspecting brands a lot of late. What's *your* excuse, seeing your boss said he meant to sell hours ago?"

Willy smiled sheepishly and confessed, "A man likes to keep abreast on current wages along the Ogallala Trail. Ain't no way you're ever gonna get your own boss to admit you might make more riding for another outfit. But it seems I've suspected Uncle John needless and it's cold as a dead witch's tits out here where the north wind can get at you. So why don't I walk you back to town and buy you a drink, or vice versa after you send that wire?"

Parson Price laughed and said, "I'd be proud to buy *you* that drink but it's too late of a Saturday to wire anybody about anything. Like I told your boss, earlier, nobody's likely to wire anybody this side of Monday."

As he nodded *adios* at the ride he'd been jawing with and fell in step at the con man's side, Willy asked in a deceptively casual tone, "How come? It's my understanding Western Union stays open for beeswax all around the clock, seven days a week, in towns of any size."

The fake Longarm explained, "The wires may be up and running, but all banks and government offices will have closed until Monday by now."

Willy insisted, "Wouldn't anybody you wired get any of the messages you have to send earlier if they were on the wires at this instant, say at night letter rates to be sent during the slack hours of the weekend, held by Western Union until business hours resume, come Monday, and delivered *poco tiempo*? You surely don't mean to hold Uncle John's bond whilst you only commence to check out his herd as distant in the future as fucking Monday morning, do you?"

"I sent a night letter about those Cherokee cows before noon, at night letter rates," the con man replied in a desperately calm tone, adding, "It's still likely to take Western Union as late as Monday noon to get word either way from the Cherokee Tribal Council. What are you and your Uncle John so worried about? Are you suggesting I might try to *keep* as big a wad as sixteen hundred dollars, for Pete's sake?"

"The thought never crossed my mind," the wirey Tex-Mex replied with a crooked smile, adding, "Why don't we just make sure you sent that night letter to Tahlequah, like you said. They'd still have it on file at Western Union, right?"

As the two of them trudged on in the bitter sunny cold, Parson Price said, "They would, but no offense, Western Union ain't about to let you read messages sent by others. Death-bed orders from Mr. Cornell, who unionized all them competing telegraph companies in the first place."

Willy nodded but insisted, "They'd let *you* read the very telegram you filled out for them earlier, wouldn't they? They'd surely have a copy to be held until such time as Tahlequah verified they'd recieved your night letter, and they won't be sending many night letters until it's darker than this."

As they got out of the wind betwixt buildings closer to the depot up the tracks from the stockyards, Parson Price said, gruffly, "I'm not so sure I cotton to your attitude, Willy. I got better things to do this afternoon than to pester Western Union about already transacted beeswax."

Willy said, "No, you don't. It'll only take a minute, and I can make out that black and yellow Western Union sign from here. So would you care to satisfy my soul or would you rather I tell Uncle John you never wired shit about his beef or that handsome bond?"

He treated them to another two paces before he added, "We rode up this way with a fair-sized crew, all bearing arms lest somebody try to get at Uncle John's beef, or Uncle John's money belt."

Parson Price growled, "Put your money where your mouth is, then. I got a hundred to one saying I can prove I wired Tahlequah about them brands this morning, and the betting starts with ten dollars at your end. For like I said, I've better things to do than run around town in circles when it's as cold outside as this!"

As he'd hoped, Willy hesitated. Ten dollars was a serious bet to a rider drawing fifty-and-found as a small-holder's *segundo*, if Uncle John Watts was paying Willy white man's wages. But the rider had sand in his craw. "You're on, and for both our sakes, I surely hope I lose. I just hate it when they put me in jail until Uncle John can get my bail and find me a good lawyer."

Parson Price snorted in disgust and suggested they get on down to Western Union and settle the sucker bet. It was easy to sound disgusted when you were so much smarter than the marks the Good Lord had created to be fleeced. *Suspicious* marks were easiest of all to think circles around.

The two of them sashayed into the cozy warmth of the Western Union and the clerk behind the counter naturally recalled the customer he'd served just that morning. He put up no argument when Parson Price told him he wanted to make sure he'd penciled one of those cattle brands in right. He produced the block-lettered two page message the con man had sent to Tahlequah in the Indian Territory early at night letter rates, knowing nobody there would reply before he and Zilphia were long gone, and knowing it was best to cover all the bases one could at low cost when conning armed and dangerous marks.

The armed and dangerous Willy Cruz proved himself a sport after he read the officious night letter signed by a federal lawman. He smiled sort of weary, and dug under his sheepskins with one hand whilst he handed the form back, saying, "I was worried needless, and I'm glad for the both of us."

Then he handed over a gold eagle, adding, "My apologies, sir, and now I mean to buy you that drink."

Parson Price handed the form across the counter to the clerk as he replied, "Just one round then, both ways, in my hotel tap room. Like I said, I've other things to do, and I'd have worn my fucking overcoat had I known this blue norther was going to settle in for keeps, this early in the fall."

Willy didn't ask if "Longarm's" other business was

35

pretty. One of Uncle John's other riders had already established "Longarm" was shacked up with a well-rounded blonde at that hotel just down the way. It was duck-soup simple to establish such things by betting a hotel maid two bits she didn't know.

When they got to his hotel, Parson Price told Cruz to wait downstairs in the lobby whilst he went on up to get that fucking overcoat. Willy didn't suggest he kiss her once for himself. He just said, "Make it snappy, then. Soon as we drink to it I got to scout Uncle John up and tell him he was worried needless."

Then he found an overstuffed chair beneath a paper palm tree to wait in the lobby as the taller man in thinner duds went upstairs for what he promised would only be a minute.

Rejoining Zilphia on the second floor, the con man told her, "Start packing. Put this wad in under your unmentionables. There's a train that's leaving for Omaha and points east just after sundown, when the light outside will be tricky."

As she took the thick roll of paper money from her lover, Zilphia asked, "Didn't you say we might score a few more stings tomorrow, on the Sabbath, before we had to leave, darling?"

He said, "That was then. Folk in our line have to change plans now and again as they think on the move. I have a suspicious mark waiting in the lobby as we speak. While you pack up here, I'll be lulling him down in the tap room. Soon as I get shed of him, I'll get back to you for some billing and cooing 'til it's safe to leave by the back door. You got to know when to discreetly leave the table in this game, and I would say the time has come, here in Ogallala."

So they kissed on it and Parson Price went back down to spoon-feed Cruz some more bullshit.

Willy wasn't waiting for Parson Price in the lobby. He

36

wasn't in the next-door taproom, either. He'd ducked out back to take a piss and he'd been shaking the dew off his lilly when the man he waited for passed by his empty chair. So that's where he was still seated when Parson Price bellied up to the bar next door, searching images in the back bar's mirror as he idly wondered where that fucking Cruz might be.

The Double W hadn't been the only gents in town who knew how to get information out of hotel maids. As Parson Price ordered the shot of Maryland rye the real Longarm was said to favor, three gents he had never seen before, all three dressed the same in cheap wool suits and brown derbies, got up from a corner table as one to advance on him like the three musketeers. But even as the con man tensed, one of them said, "Pinkerton Agent Reynolds, here. Ain't you Custis Long, as rides for our Uncle Sam?"

When Parson Price confessed he might be, the real Oregon Bob replied with a delighted smile, "Henderson and Winslow, here, would be backing my play. I'll bet all four of us are here in Ogallala after that same bank robbing son of a bitch, Lefty Lindwood, right?"

Parson Price knew about trick questions. He asked a lot of them. So he said, "Maybe I am and maybe I ain't. But I'm pleased to meet you just the same."

Then the damn fool held out his gun hand to shake, and from there, it all went easier than expected, up to one unexpected point.

As the man they took for the real Longarm shook with Oregon Bob, Giggles to the left of him and Weedy to the right of him exchanged knowing glances and slapped leather as one.

Parson Price only had time to gasp, "Hold on! You boys have nothing to worry about!" before they both fired, and kept firing, as Parson Price melted like candle wax

37

into the sawdust on the floor with one dead hand still firmly grasped by Oregon Bob.

Then another bullet went in one ear and out the other of the killer called Giggles when Willy Cruz fired from the archway to the hotel lobby before he'd had time to yell, "What the fuck?"

Weedy Dorn got to hear the angry question just before another round took him over the heart while he stood there with an empty six-gun and egg on his face.

But Oregon Bob had yet to draw his Schofield .45 with five in the wheel and he got it out just in time as Cruz fired through the thick gunsmoke at him to miss him by a whisker.

Then Cruz went down with his smoking gun waving and a .45-28 slug in his own hasty heart to leave nobody but the barkeep and Oregon Bob on their feet.

The barkeep didn't think it wise to ask a stranger with a smoking Schofield why he'd just taken part in the killings of four other gents. So he dropped limp as a dishrag behind the thick mahogany bar to commence crawling along the duckboards to where he'd put his own sawed-off ten guage.

By the time he got to it and risked a wary peek over the top of the bar, the taproom was empty, save for the haze of brimstone-scented gun smoke and those four bodies spread across the sawdust.

So the balding barkeep got to his feet and placed the ten guage on the bar in front of him, and it was found that way by the first Ogallala lawman who tore in out of the cold, responding to the dulcet tones of gunplay with his own Colt '73 in hand.

Taking in the scene at a glance, the town law gasped, "Jesus H! This scene reminds me of the last act of *Hamlet*! What happened, Doc?"

As the barkeep told him, the town law hunkered low to pat bodies down for identification. Since Doc had just said the tall one in the tweed suit had seemed the intended victim, the town law searched the corpse of Parson Price first, to stare up with a look of sheer wonder as he waved the dead man's wallet, saying, "Bleating wolves and howling sheep if these as-yet-to-be-identified murderous rascals ain't just now murdered the famous federal lawman known as Longarm!"

Chapter 5

The real Longarm's desk-bound boss, Marshal Billy Vail, had by then gotten good at cutting sign on paper as he'd once cut sign on the Staked Plains in his pre-war hitch in the Texas Rangers. They wouldn't let him man his cluttered desk at the Denver federal building on the officious day of rest, but the old-timer who just loved the game had a standing agreement with Western Union, seeing they had a lot of wire strung across federal range, to deliver any wires sent to him of a Sunday at his private address up on Capitol Hill.

So once they'd delivered a mighty impolite message from his opposite number over to Ogallala, Nebraska, for land's sake, Billy almost sent the messenger boy to Longarm's rooming house on the less fashionable side of Cherry Creek before he remembered Longarm would be showing up for inspection at Judge Dickerson's brownstone, to the other side of the nearby Colorado statehouse, no later than three P.M.

So when Longarm showed up that cold dry afternoon, he had to smile at the contrast the two older men made as they gathered in the kitchen, where men could talk without worrying about their ashes or spilled liquid re-

41

freshments. For, even seated at the kitchen table, the contrast betwixt the tall, lean judge and the short, stubby marshal was sort of amusing.

They allowed Longarm looked funny as hell, too, gussied up like a riverboat gambler who pimped on the side. Billy Vail swore that in all his days along the border, he'd never seen such a ridiculous Spanish hat as that one before.

When Judge Dickerson opined it seemed a shame Longarm wasn't going to get to wear such an outfit to Leavenworth after all, Longarm asked how come.

Billy Vail explained, "Lefty Lindwood ain't in Leavenworth. He just murdered you in Ogallala and their marshal over yonder was sore as all hell at us for sending one of our own into his jurisdiction without a word of explanation."

As Judge Dickerson's pretty "niece" poured a cup to go, with the marble cake in front of Longarm, Billy continued, "I just wired him we never sent you or anybody else to poke about his neck of the woods for anybody. Then, the judge, here, issued a carte blanche court order good from border to border and, if need be, beyond."

Judge Dickerson nodded and said, "Your new orders, Deputy Long, are to leave at once for Ogallala and, with or without the cooperation of the local law, catch up with Lefty Lindwood, arrest him for ordering the murder of whomsoever they just murdered, and ask him who in blue blazes they just murdered!"

Billy Vail explained, "Until he gets my return night letter in the morning, he'll go on thinking you were the victim, because the man on the taproom floor was found to have nine bullets in him and the badge and ID one would expect to find on Deputy U.S. Marshal Custis Long of our Denver District Court. The only surviving witness, a barkeep, told 'em three jaspers wearing identical derbies addressed their victim by name and that he admitted he

42

was you before one held his gun hand for him whilst the other two pumped him full of lead!"

Longarm whistled and said, "I'll bet that smarted! But how do they know I was murdered by Lefty Lindwood, boss?"

Vail said, "Two of them wound up on the same tap-room floor and the town law was able to backtrack 'em to the hotel they'd been staying at with the one who got away, two gals, and a skull-faced individual who signed the register left-handed. One of the dead gang members worked as the known associate called Giggles Gleason. The other was almost surely the late Weedy Dorn, and the barkeep allowed he was sure the one as got away had a red moustache, adding up pretty good to Oregon Bob Cooke."

Longarm sipped some black coffee thoughtfully and asked how he might have taken two of his killers with him, seeing Oregon Bob was hanging on his gun hand.

Vail said, "You had a pal they weren't expecting. No mystery about him. His name was Guillhermo or Willy Cruz. He rode up from Texas with an honest outfit known as the Double W. The way we've put her together, so far, Cruz had come to the hotel to talk with you or whoever in hell he was about some federal bond. I'm still working on what they were talking about. Cruz was coming in from the lobby as the three derby hats threw down on . . . whoever. Cruz naturally threw down on them, and the barkeep thinks it was the redhead who blew Cruz away whilst Cruz took out his two pals."

Longarm smiled thinly and said, "Sounds noisy. What happened next?"

Billy Vail said, "After they identified the real Willy Cruz and an obvious imposter pretending to be you, they patted the dead killers down to discover fake private detective licenses and a pair of Pinkerton badges lost, strayed or stolen, according to the Pinks. They say they've

43

never had no private ops called Agent Henderson and Agent Winslow in the habit of shooting gents down in cold-ass blood like so!"

Vail wet his own whistle with somewhat stronger stuff before he went on, "After that, both the dead derby hats were packing tagged room keys from the same hotel just down the way. All this patting down and jawing back and forth took some time, of course. So, by the time the town law got to said hotel, the others who'd been staying yonder with the two dead men had left without bothering to check out. No trains nor coaches had left town betwixt the shooting and the posting of town deputies at all the most likely ways to leave town. That's not saying nobody could have got away on foot or even on horseback. Albeit none of the liveries in town offer any help with that angle. So they're betting, and we agree, the surviving members of the gang are holed up somewhere else, right there in Ogallala. It's a fair-sized railroad town with plenty of strange faces moving about at all hours."

Judge Dickerson chimed in, "Lefty Lindwood is a habitual criminal. The bunch he led up to Nebraska add up to habitual criminals. They must have headed for Ogallala with some crime in mind. Why would Lefty feel he had to run that far, seeing neither Giggles nor Weedy are about to talk and Oregon Bob got away clean after killing the only supposed lawman in those parts who might know Lefty Lindwood on sight?"

Longarm almost asked a dumb question. Then he nodded and said, "I'd say that adds up to a sensible motive, if whoever was pretending to be me had the gang convinced he might be! Has anybody come up with any sensible motive for *that* wild claim, gents?"

Vail said, "The cuss they shot in your place might have been a con man. The town law is still working on that, out around the stockyards. It seems before he was murdered in the taproom of his own hotel, the tall drink of water whose moustache turned out to be as fake as his badge had been demanding bond money on suspicious brands. You know how that tiresome sting works, don't you, Custis?"

Longarm nodded wearily and said, "I'm surprised some drovers still go for it. How much money did they recover?"

Vail said, "Not much. They learned, too late, he'd been staying with a woman upstairs. Time they got around to tossing his hired room, neither she nor even the hotel towels were there. She describes as a brassy blonde the room service help found bossy. Show me a transient hotel in this land of the free as doesn't have at least one brassy, bossy blonde on their guest list and I'll show you a hotel where business has been slow!"

Judge Dickerson said, "Never mind that drifting pair of flimflams. Extorting whatever out of local suckers, however they might have done it, constitutes a local offense for Nebraska, not us, to worry about."

Longarm kept his thoughts to himself as the fair but sometime awfully firm older lawman went on, "Their only worth to us, whoever they might have been, is that mistaking a con man for a lawman who knew him on sight inspired Lefty Lindwood to break cover and, better yet, move on the double to cover that may not be as good. So here are my new orders. Get out of that clown suit, get yourself over to Ogallala, then report to Marshal Fender, yonder, as your true self."

Vail chimed in, "They'll know by the time you get there that somebody else was gunned down in your place. You might make better time if you hopped this afternoon's Overland Stage out of Tremont Place to Nebraska by way of Julesburg. Slower but more direct across the plains and leaving hours before the night train takes you to that layover near the Kansas line, see?"

"How come?" asked Longarm, adding, "And I don't

45

mean how come the stage through Julesburg. I can see that's the most direct route. I mean how come you want me to report to anyone alive and well in Ogallala, seeing as Lefty Lindwood, if that's who had me murdered, thinks I'm dead?"

Vail snorted, "Thunderation, old son, how long do you think such a stupid mistake will stay out of the local papers, once Marshal Fender gets the night letter I just sent him?"

Longarm said, "Not long, I fear. But ain't it possible to take back a telegram before it can be delivered, seeing you were the one who paid to send the dumb message in the first place?"

The two older lawmen exchanged glances as the young thing cutting cake on the sideboard decided she was wasting her time and desisted.

Billy Vail said, "Anything's possible, if Western Union knows what an irate federal official can do to a small-town clerk who sasses him. But what was so dumb about us assuring Marshal Fender, the local law and the newspapers all over that the small-time crook they killed was not the real Custis Long, shaking down cowhands for drinking money?"

Judge Dickerson nodded and threw in, "We hardly want it said that any officer of the Denver District Court was a petty crook!"

Longarm insisted, "I don't mind what some may say about me as long as I'm *dead*. I'd rather everybody, including those crooks we're after, have me down as dead and, hell, *disgraced*, if that inspires old Jethro Lefty Lindwood to a false sense of security!"

Billy Vail said, "Hot damn! Sorry, ma'am! Are you saying Lindwood may break cover some more if he thinks you're still dead?"

Longarm had tried a nibble of cake while Billy was talking. It was too sweet and a tad stale. He washed it down with a hasty sip and told his boss, "I doubt they holed up all that serious, once Oregon Bob got back to assure them the only cuss in town who could identify Lefty was dead. The derby hats and wool suits on the dead pards Oregon Bob left behind were no doubt disguises. By the time they'd packed to leave the one hotel, Oregon Bob would have changed and he might have shaved that red face hair."

Judge Dickerson brightened and said, "I follow your drift. The sneaky rascals could be hiding out in plain sight, within a pistol shot of that one transient hotel!"

Vail chortled, "I told you he was good, Your Honor. Marshal Fender may never forgive me. But I've all night to rephrase the night letter he'll be reading on a blue Monday morn."

Cocking a brow at Longarm, Vail added, "I've a mind to say we are sorry as anything a man from our court with a serious drinking problem and some heavy gambling debts went over to Ogallala on his own to see if he could take unfair advantage of the fall beef sales by abusing his own badge!"

Longarm nodded and declared, "That ought to work and, better yet, if Denver sends for my body, embalmed on rock salt in a sealed lead box, no nosey newpaper reporter who knows my face would be able to give our show away. They ought to handle it the way they did the murder of poor old James Butler Hickok, shot by another drunk in the Number Ten Saloon to be rehabilitated as the noble Wild Bill, frontier lawman and master of the Great Plains. Just so Lefty and what's left of his gang have me down as nobody to worry about when I show up in this fool outfit as a knock-around flash called Frank Mason. I picked the phony name because it's a play on Freemason as soon as anyone sneaky studies on it."

"Hold on. You're missing something scary!" Billy Vail cut in, adding, "Your clever ploy only works to one possibly fatal point, old son. You know Lefty Lindwood on sight because you beat him up and arrested him that time. Don't you suppose it possible he'd be as inclined to recognize *you* at this late date?"

Longarm said, "Up close and whispering words of endearment in his shell-like ear, no doubt. But he's a funny looking cuss who stands out in a smoke-filled saloon whilst I'm just young and beautiful. Thanks to the infernal newspaper reporters describing me all over the place, that con man pretending to be me wore my usual Stetson and that sissy suit you and President Hayes have had me wearing on duty. Walking up the slope from Broadway, just now, I caught myself by surprise in more than one shop window and wondered who that bird might be before I saw it was my own reflection!"

He saw Vail needed more convincing and insisted, "I don't need to be taken on Lefty Lindwood's knee as a long-lost child, boss. I only have to get close enough to spot him *first*. Once I do, I'll see if I can get the drop on him and take him alive. Once I take him alive, I can bring him back to you and I ain't sure you want me to know the deal you may have to offer him in exchange for those names you really want!"

He could tell by the older man's stern expression he'd guessed right.

When Dickerson mused, "It's not as if we can *prove* he ordered the death of that otherwise worthless con man . . ." Longarm managed not to cuss in front of the lady. He knew how his world was really run and he'd long since given up trying to change it. He knew he was too soft-hearted to pack a badge. But after growing up on a hard-scrabble hill farm in West-By-God Virginia and trying other jobs such as digging mines and driving beef, Longarm figured he'd never get a better job than the one he had, and all honest toil left calluses.

He suspected gents like Judge Dickerson might have

started out with softer hearts, only to learn, the hard way, a man did what he had to do in the name of the law and tough shit to them who got trampled by not paying attention where they were headed.

So the three of them agreed to Longarm's plan, with the reservation that all the blame would be on his own plate if things blew up in his face over Ogallala way.

Billy Vail's surrey was tethered out front and so, seeing he had to get on down to Western Union for some discussion about night letters, his boss gave Longarm and his sissy carpetbag a ride down Colfax as far as Tremont Place, near the intersection of Colfax and Broadway, where one caught the Overland Stage along the South Platte up to Julesburg near the Colorado-Nebraska line.

A couple of others in the Overland waiting room shot curious looks at the flashy outfit Longarm had on that afternoon. But nobody said a thing calling for a fight until an all-too-familiar figure in a checked suit that flashed some in its own right shot a second glance at Longarm, laughed like hell, and declared, "I give up! You and the other kids couldn't wait for the end of the month, so you're holding your Halloween costume party this evening?"

Longarm grabbed Reporter Crawford of the *Denver Post* by one arm to haul him outside, out of earshot, as he warned, "You're in line for an exclusive, before the end of the month you just mentioned, or a punch in the nose and at least seventy-two hours on suspicion in the Federal House of Detention, Crawford. So which might you prefer?"

Reporter Crawford whistled and replied, "That important, eh? I have your word I get the story first, once you want the headlines to run?"

Longarm said, "You do, provided you'll help us out with an earlier white lie in the cause of justice."

So Reporter Crawford allowed they had a deal and by

49

the time the flashy Frank Jones checked into the Ogallala Overland Rest, Monday afternoon, it was out on the news service wires that the notorious Frank Mason, a vaguely sinister young man with no visible means of support, had shot a man in Denver in the thigh before leaving town in a hurry lest the good sport who'd declined to press charges go and die on him.

Chapter 6

The real Longarm had chosen the hotel the fake Longarm had been staying at because he had to check in somewhere and because it would seem more natural to ask casual questions about the shooting in their taproom if he had a good excuse for being on the premises.

He wound up in Room 2-F for the simple reason that the flashy blonde who'd been there last had left that room for rent without checking out.

Longarm didn't cotton to sailing that close to the wind, but he knew he'd raise as many or more eyebrows by letting on he had some call to *avoid* the freshly swept and tidied-up quarters the mysterious blonde had been sharing with the famous lawman murdered downstairs. He was hardly surprised when none of the hotel help said he looked at all like the famous Longarm, seeing they'd all likely known the imposter as the same, before and after he'd been spread out across the sawdust with those other gents last Saturday night.

Longarm knew better than to ask around town about the disposal of his famous corpse. The local undertaker Billy Vail would have wired by now would have shipped it in a sealed coffin by this time if he knew what was good for him. None of the three local papers Longarm had treated himself to down in the lobby had mentioned that fake moustache or any other false notes suggesting there might have been a dumb mistake down yonder. So Billy's reworded night letter appeared to have warned the local law not to offer any embarrassing details about a lawman gone wrong. Marshal Fender had suggested some cattlemen who'd come to him with tangled tales about posting bonds with the late Deputy Long had best take the confusion up with their lawyers, since he was way more interested in the killer who'd gotten away after gunning a federal man than he was in rumors of financial irregularities that hardy sounded all that federal.

Having given his travel dust time to settle, Longarm left his hired Room 2-F for an early supper just a tad after five P.M. He was really hungry and anxious now to let them get used to his strange face and flashy duds around that part of town.

Remembering how Reporter Crawford and that pesky Ned Buntline had gone into the personal habits of their famous Longarm as they bullshit a heap about other details, Longarm ordered the blue-plate special that was on the menu in the hotel dining room, across the lobby from that wing that held their taproom. He'd have gone for chili over a T-bone, without those limp, gray string beans, for God's sake, had he been more free to order. But yet another fucking reporter had repeated his own words about chili con carne getting less hot as one moved north or south of the Mexican border and he'd given up his three-for-a-nickel cheroots on this mission as well. And he just wasn't up to those expensive but odious cigars Billy Vail had offered back in Denver.

It made him grimace, but that evening he put a shot of cream and a spoonful of sugar in his coffee, the way most soft-living jaspers were inclined to take their java. It hurt like hell to pass on the berry pie in favor of chocolate layer cake. But he managed.

Nobody in the nearly empty hotel restaurant seemed to notice his sacrifices. But he knew it was when you felt least watched that somebody might be watching you and the chocolate cake wasn't bad. If only they hadn't had berry pie on the menu.

Strolling across the lobby and into the taproom, Longarm found no company at the bar that early. The balding barkeep said they called him Doc and asked Mr. "Jones" what he was having.

Longarm ordered bourbon instead of rye with the usual draft chaser, thanks to that pesky Reporter Crawford naming every damn brand but his shaving soap in that one interview.

He knew better than to let on he'd heard somebody had been shot at this very bar he was standing at. Recent. He was in there early to let Doc establish him as familiar, not as a Nosey Parker who'd just blown in out of the cold, asking questions.

They talked about the blue norther outside. Doc allowed they usually blew over, one way or the other, in three days or less. Longarm agreed they'd either get warmed up or snowed in before long. Then, as he'd hoped, Doc casually asked if he was staying in the hotel.

Longarm allowed he was, adding nothing as to what he might be doing in a transient town, dressed so flashy. Wiping the bar and looking off at nothing much, Doc casually made mention of the friendly game in that one far corner, most week nights, starting around eight.

He added, "That's about the time most Mexicans have supper and the regulars tend to wager like white men, if you know what I mean."

Longarm, aka Frank Jones or Frank Mason, shrugged and said he knew what Doc meant. Then he said, "I've sworn off friendly games with total strangers for a spell.

53

Had a little trouble a few nights back with such a cuss. They say he'll live. But I'd as soon be accused of fucking my mother than marking a fresh deck."

Doc nodded in a satisfied manner and replied, "Then I take it it was on the money about you being a sporting man, Mr. Jones?"

Longarm swilled some suds, put the schooner down half full, and put some edge in his voice as he replied in a colder tone, "You just heard me say I've sworn off for now. Are you writing a book, Doc? Or are you just a nosey . . . Never mind."

Then he turned on one heel and stomped out as, behind him, the barkeep called, "Hold on, Mr. Jones! I wasn't trying to pry! I was just being friendly! Come back here and have the next one on the house!"

Longarm kept going, satisfied Doc would be talking about him with the regulars before he let any of them talk to him. He considered an early stroll around town before sundown but it was cold as hell outside and he decided to go back up to Room 2-F and haul that pea coat out of his carpetbag, first.

There was plenty of daylight left, with a window at the far end of the hall. So Longarm could see the match stem on the hall runner long before he got to the door he'd locked after him earlier.

The match stem had been wedged under the bottom hinge of the door as he'd locked up, as was his wont, with such moments as this in mind. That match stem had fallen to the runner when the door had been opened, sneaky, by somebody else whilst he was out.

Reaching under his lavender frock coat for his .44-40, Longarm started to reach for the knob with his free hand. Then he had an easier notion as he listened sharp to the considerable disturbance on the far side of the thin wood paneling.

Whoever it was wasn't going through the few possibles

54

in the one carpetbag. The prowler was opening and shutting the drawers of the end table or dresser. Longarm knew that either way there were a finite number of drawers to toss. So he flattened against the wall outside the door for just a spell and, sure enough, things quieted down. Then the door popped ajar and a gal stuck her head out to peer up and down the hopefully empty hallway.

She'd looked the other way first. So the muzzle of Longarm's double action six-gun was almost touching her nose when she swung it his way, gasped, and tried to crawfish back inside with her weight against the door to slam it shut.

But seeing Longarm had fifty pounds or more on her, she and the door both flew inwards as he shouldered hard and chased his leveled gun muzzle in after them.

He could see right off the gal had landed on her ass on the rug near the bed and she had both empty hands braced against the rug. So Longarm stepped in, kicked the door shut and said, "Your servant, ma'am. Looking for something you might have lost around here?"

She snapped, "I'm not a sneak thief, damn your eyes!" and he liked her spunk. So Longarm moved in to extend his free hand and help her to her feet as he looked her over some more.

It didn't hurt. She was somewhere in her late twenties or early thirties, dressed fashionably but sedate in maroon Dolly Varden skirts and a matching, tightly-tailored bodice. There was enough give in her torso as he helped her up to establish her narrow waist was natural.

After that, her oval face was blushing and she kept looking away from him with those big, hot, chocolate eyes. Her upswept hair, worn in a corona braid across the top of her aristocratic skull, was the color of fresh-pulled taffy. Her tits weren't bad, either.

He figured since she wasn't dressed for the blue norther outside, she'd snuck into his room from another in the

55

same hotel. She confirmed his suspicion by trying, "I must be on the wrong floor. Isn't this Room 3-E?"

Longarm held on to her hand and never put his .44-40 away, albeit he pointed it at the floor, saying, "You'll have to do better than that, ma'am. I locked that door as I went out a short spell back. The key is in my possession. It ain't supposed to be in yours. So would you care to explain to the house detective or would you rather explain to me? I've already figured you weren't after anything in that carpetbag on that dresser. I haven't unpacked it yet. So nothing of mine would be in any of those drawers you were opening and shutting. How do you like it so far?"

She smiled wearily to answer, "I might have known, seeing you got to this room ahead of me. Who are you operating for, Pinkerton or the Met?"

He walked into the tender trap she'd set, replying, "I'm neither an insurance nor a railroad dick and weren't we about to reveal who in thunder you might be, ma'am?"

She answered easily, "Salome Morrigan, working out of Omaha for the Bancroft Agency. You'd be a bounty hunter operating on his own, huh?"

"I never said so," Longarm replied, truthfully enough.

She went on holding hands with him, and it was commencing to get sort of sweaty, as she wrinkled her pert nose to answer, "They told me down at the desk that a Mr. Jones had already booked the room I asked for, and I like the cover story you planted on the news wire to go with that tinhorn flash. You're never going to collect any bounty on the late Parson Price nor the incarcerated Zilphia La Belle. But there could still be something in it for you if you'd care to throw in with me."

Longarm holstered his six-gun, reeled her in for a kiss, and allowed he was listening.

After kissing back, French, the taffy blonde pushed free with a laugh to say, "Down, boy! I was talking about *money*! As we speak, the more willing Zilphia La Belle languishes in an Omaha jail cell because when I went over to make her bail she refused to tell me where the rest of the money was. She swore she didn't know what I was talking about, the naughty girl. But all she had on her when the railroad dicks took her off at the U.P. Terminal in Omaha, kicking and screaming, was a tad over eighteen hundred dollars."

"*Whose* eighteen hundred dollars?" Longarm asked.

Salome said, "More than one cattle outfit, she admitted. She and the late Parson Price spent some recent time in this very room, with him going over to the stockyards, pretending to be that famous lawman they call Longarm, when he wasn't spending time with Zilphia in that very bed!"

"Are you saying what I just read in the papers about somebody killing Longarm in this same hotel the other night is . . . ?"

"A pile of doggy doo!" she nodded, adding, "Lord knows why the *real* Longarm hasn't set them straight by this late in the game."

He suggested, "Mayhaps he don't know he's dead, yet. Have you told anyone else here in Ogallala the true name of the cadaver down in the taproom?"

She shrugged and asked, "Why should I? I paid for my education. Let them pay for theirs. I understand the Pinks asked the Omaha P.D. to keep a lid on it after they got his brassy blonde to tell them just about everything but where the rest of the money was."

He smiled down, bemused. She said, "To keep his killers off base, of course. If Parson Price never hid the money from his sweet Zilphia the killers might have it and the Met's paying a handsome finder's fee for its recovery."

"You mean you might not be the only undercover cop me and the ones who gunned down such a rich lawman have to worry about?"

She sniffed, "If they knew he had that much money, they knew he wasn't the real Longarm. It's easy enough to see how they guessed. Before he was shot downstairs he was out at the stockyards, posing as the law and demanding bond money lest he interfere in the hot and heavy trading out yonder. Zilphia La Belle insists all she saw was the wad of centuries and ten spots she said he'd pressed on her for safekeeping. But as soon as he lay dead downstairs, the stockmen he'd shaken down for bond money came forward, asking about the same."

She leaned closer to confide in a lower tone, "Even if some of them are drawing the long bow to account for cash in their own back pockets, we figure Parson Price had conned at least five thousand before someone put a stop to his sting with malice aforethought. There could be more and, as we've just established, I'm better at searching baggage and drawers than knocking people down. So why don't we team up?"

Longarm wanted no such deal. He wanted the pretty little thing who knew too much on the next train back to Omaha. So he said they had a deal, reeled her in, and kissed her dirtier as he got a left-handed grip on her firm little ass.

It didn't work as planned. She tried, "For heaven's sake, it's too early to fool around like that, Frank!"

To which he replied with a firmer grip, "Who's fooling? I spent last night setting up aboard a bumpy stage with my pants on and it's the pure simple truth that you're the best looking thing I've seen since leaving Denver!"

He'd suspected she'd chosen her own phony name with the tempting Princess Salome and the sneaky, shape-shifting Morrigan of Irish myths in mind. She proved that whoever she was she didn't scare off easy by simply smiling up at him like a good sport to say, "Only if I have your word we'll be putting our heads together, for some serious thinking, as soon as we settle your nerves by putting some other parts together, you naughty boy!"

Chapter 7

When a man struck gold or a great lay, he had no call to worry his poor head about past complexications of geology or who taught such a refined-looking young lady to fuck so fine. Somebody surely had, and a man enjoying the results at this late date felt better about it when he left the details blurred. So he never asked which of her previous lovers had told her she evoked those tales about the shape-shifting fey woman they called the Morrigan. He'd noticed, getting her undressed, how that fashionably tailored bodice had been concealing tits worth their weight in gold, once they popped out more natural, and it sure beat all how Dolly Varden skirts could hide the serpentine lower reaches of a born belly dancer with the legs of a prima ballerina.

Salome, if that was her name, seemed pleasantly surprised by her new-found pard's naked charms, once they were seriously swapping spit and other body fluids whilst the setting sun out yonder painted their heaving flesh and everything around them a golden glow that looked way warmer than it really was outside.

Longarm chose to believe her, it felt better, when she suddenly let loose with, "Oh, my God! I think I'm going to *come* with you! What are you *doing* to me, you naughty boy?"

He just went on doing it, resisting the obvious opportunity to answer dirty. He was enjoying her more than he'd expected to. But he wanted to get shed of her, not to tie himself down with a clinging vine who liked a man to talk dirty to her.

Longarm liked women, as fellow human beings, and hence he inclined to screw 'em the way they liked to be screwed, knowing how Dame Nature had stacked the deck against satisfactory screwing so's all creation would screw frustrated and often as possible instead of the way those poets suggested.

Having taken the time to study one of his favorite subjects in and out of bed with the help of some medical books and this army nurse he would always remember fondly, Longarm knew men and women deserved more than either could give the other, screwing natural. The trick was not to screw a pal exactly the way you naturally *wanted* to screw her. That army nurse had drawn him a sort of graph on the steamed up window glass of her cozy bedroom window a few nights before Christmas, long ago and far away. The diagram of she-male desire sort of resembled the trajectory of an artillery shell, with the gal's feelings getting warmer and warmer in a smooth climb to her climax and as smooth on her glide back down unless the idiot fucking her messed up and they wound up with a dud as never went anywhere.

The curve that understanding army nurse said a *man's* desires followed wasn't smooth at all. He went from behaving his fool self to a raging hard-on at an incline way steeper than gals got hot, to be huffing and puffing like a raging bull by the time they were ready to let him feel some titty. And many a gal who'd about decided "maybe" could spook and run off to pleasure herelf less scary when a rider gave her too much of the quirt before she was ready to lope.

But a man who'd mastered his raging bulls had an advantage on the lucky few who managed to steal into home plate to just wiggle natural at the risk of leaving the poor gal halfways up her own natural peak of pleasure.

For when a man could rein his own galloping desires in enough to bounce in the old love saddle as if he was loping his way home to supper, instead of riding for his life, he could last as he drove her desires ever hotter and higher, as he seemed to be doing at the moment with old Salome until she gasped, "Oh, no, Jesus! I'm coming *again!*" and Longarm suspected he might have been over-considerate.

So he put his back into it to come himself, which inspired her to moan, "Stop! I can't take any more and . . . don't stop . . . I think I can . . . I know I can . . . and Jeeeeeeeeezussss!"

He kissed her sincerely, as any man would have at such a time, and didn't fight her as she rolled him off, sobbing, "What kind of an animal are you? What kind of an animal did you turn me into just now, you adorable freak? Don't you care anything about all that money?"

Longarm stretched, started to fumble for a cheroot to share with her before he remembered he was some other great lover, and observed, "We ain't about to find any money hidden in this room, Sal. To begin with, that con man's gal wouldn't have left it behind unless she was loco and even if she was loco the hotel help would have found it when they did this room over. Anyone can see and smell they've changed the bedding, swept the rug and dusted good."

She sat up, still flushed from orgasm but driven by cooler desires, to say, "I never looked under the rug, and who's to say they turned the mattress when they remade the bed? Get up, silly! Help me toss the fucking room!"

Longarm laughed, but rather than fuss about it, and dying for that smoke, he swung his bare feet to the rug in question, rose naked to his considerable height, and manhandled one end of the feather mattress clear of the slats as he joshed, "I'm sure I'd hide money I was holding out on a gal in a room I was fixing to check out of."

She hunkered on her naked haunches to lift one end of the rug as she insisted, "He was shot downstairs before they ever checked out. So what if you're right? What if Parson Price held back on his Zilphia up here, assuming it was safe while he went downstairs to the taproom and then . . . Oh, shit, there's nothing under this end of the rug. Help with the other end, damn it!"

Longarm let go of the mattress, hunkered down beside her and together they made sure there was nothing but wool fuzz, two toothpicks and a hairpin under the rug before they spread it flat again. Then Longarm rolled her on her back to enjoy her on the floor, or start to, before the now dusty nude shoved him away with a laugh, saying, "This is no time to show off, Frank! If Zilphia La Belle had less than half the amount the dead man conned those stockmen out of . . ."

"It ain't up here," Longarm told her, flatly, adding, "Assuming his gal had all he gave her when she was picked up in Omaha, then he never gave her half, and he never left it up here, so what's left?"

Seated beside him on the rug, Salome started to suggest something dumb about banks, then nodded soberly and decided, "He had it on him when he was shot, downstairs."

Longarm didn't answer. He brushed some dust off her sweaty shoulder and then, seeing she hadn't seemed to mind, got a better grip on her as she asked, "Who do you suspect, Frank?"

Longarm rose to seat her on the edge of the bed. Turning from her to fetch a damp washcloth from the corner stand, he shrugged his bare shoulders to ask, "You want 'em alphabetical or numerical? According to the barkeep, Parson Price just lay there a spell with nobody going through his pockets *official* before the town law arrived."

As he wiped her down, Salome said, "The barkeep could have done it before anyone else came in. If the town law didn't do it, any number of hands in the crowd could have slipped a wad, or a money belt, under his own coattails in the confusion."

Tossing the washcloth aside to kiss her refreshed nipple, Longarm said, "That's about the size of it, Sal. We're talking about uncertain amounts of nondescript cash, whether paper or specie. No way to tell who might have it now, right?"

She lay back and welcomed him back with spread thighs as she languidly insisted her agency would want her to report on any locals suddenly spending more than they'd ever had to spend before.

He just mounted up again to spend himself in her some more without pointing to the fatal flaw in her fable. If she wanted to think she had him thinking she was out to recover money for an insurance company, so be it. He had no call to point out there was no way in hell to insure *money* and as long as they were having so much fun bullshitting one another, he didn't go into the spending habits of knock-around gents in a boomtown during the fall beef sales. He just allowed he might mosey about the card houses and saloons of Ogallala to see if he could get a line on any reports of sudden wealth. For as swell as she screwed, the night was young and he knew they hadn't sent him all this way to do nothing but screw big fibbers.

So they ended up dog style in the gathering dusk, and she said it just wasn't fair that unescorted gals weren't supposed to go nosing around card houses and saloons after dark. He swore he'd report to her up in 3-E the minute he caught anybody flashing unusual amounts of cash they couldn't account for. He wondered if that sounded as dumb to her as it did to him. But it was getting late and he had to get cracking.

Across the way, Phoebe Blake was staked out in that chili parlor as Longarm pulled down the shade and lit the bed lamp in 2-F to clean up and get dressed some more.

Lefty had told her to keep an eye on the hotel and report on what the law might be doing about the killing of his old enemy, Longarm.

As far as Phoebe could tell, they hadn't been doing anything at all interesting. Someone had just lit a lamp in the room the late lawman had been staying in with that gal. They'd told her when she'd struck up a conversation with a hotel maid at suppertime that the room had been rehired to a new guest. A flashy salesman or mayhaps a sporting man, according to the maid. Pheobe didn't see what Lefty expected her to do about that. He likely wanted to be alone some more with Verona. He didn't like it when others watched him going down on Verona, the shy son of a bitch.

Not feeling up to eating anyone or anything at the moment, Longarm in the persona of Hotel Guest Frank Jones entered the taproom, alone, to wet his whistle and get his bearings as he saw, just as Doc had promised, that a friendly little game had started at that corner table. So at the barkeep's suggestion, feeling more awkward than usual in his flashy getup, Longarm drifted over, beer schooner in hand to size the local talent up.

The obvious professional, dealing with his back to the corner, smiled up at the newcomer like a spider welcoming a fly as he declared, "How do. I'm called Spats Gordon. This other distinguished looking sport to my left would be Ace Perdue. The grinning youth with cow shit on his teeth would be *Segundo* Stan off the Flying H and we call this elderly drugstore man Soda Pop. The name of the game tonight is blackjack and stakes are an affordable two bits a deal. How do you like it so far?"

Longarm smiled thinly and replied, "My game is poker. Five-card stud when I get to call her. I don't pack enough quarters as a rule to buck your average blackjack dealer, no offense."

Spats Gordon's smile faded. His hatchet face hadn't been that pretty to begin with and his piercing blue eyes narrowed nasty as he softly but firmly hissed, "The hell I ain't offended, you sarcasticated sharpy! For it seems to this child he just heard a fucking pimp in a purple hat call him a dirty dealer!"

Across the sawdust, Doc, the barkeep, called out, "Spats, I'd like a word with you in private!"

Spats snapped, "Later, Doc, after this panty-waist with a shit-eating grin and a beer in his gun hand explains what he meant by that remark about enough quarters!"

Longarm said, "Don't get your bowels in an uproar and pay attention as I repeat my observation about *average* blackjack dealers. You must have a guilty conscience if you think that makes you a dirty dealer. All I meant to imply was that your game, played straight or crooked, is both faster than poker and calls for as much luck as skill. I only meant I liked to win or lose my pocket jingle slower. But it's a free country and you gents were here first, playing as you saw fit. So I reckon I'll just get her on down the road 'til I come to games more to my fancy."

"You'd better get it on down the road, you two-bit-hoarding pimp!" snapped Spats Gordon as Doc rolled his eyes up at the pressed tin to move around the end of the bar.

Longarm moved the other way, sipping suds, to deposit his half-full schooner on the bar near the street entrance and mosey on out as, behind him, Spats Gordon crowed, "Knew the moment I laid eyes on that orange vest he had a yaller streak from his asshole to that Spanish hat!"

Thanks to the crisp autumn weather, the usual batwings had been replaced for the winter by a full door. But as Longarm paused just outside in the dark to light one of the claro cigars he was smoking as Frank Mason, he could hear Doc yelling inside, "Don't you know better than to start up with total stangers wearing hardware, Spats? Our Mr. Jones you just called a pimp is the one and original Frank Mason of the owlhoot trail!"

Longarm had to listen tighter when Spats replied in a defensive tone, "I don't care who he is and . . . who did you say he was, Doc?"

Longarm strode away, smiling thinly, as the barkeep explained how Spats had just brushed, too close for comfort, with a man on the dodge for shooting another card shark at another card table, recent. Lord love Reporter Crawford and the *Denver Post*!

Crossing the dark but not yet empty street, Longarm spied a not bad bitty brunette watching him from the front window of what sure looked like a chili parlor. It *smelled* like the same as he got closer, wishing he was somebody else, for the smell of simmering *menudons* was escaping out the vents above their door and a bowl of *menudos* with a plate of *chili verde con carne* would do wonders for a man who'd just been screwed half to death by a shape shifting fey woman.

But that same reporter who'd described the armed and dangerous Frank Mason so well had told everyone how the famous Longarm smoked cheroots and lived on tortillas and *menudos* like a damned Mex. So when Longarm got to the far side, he only cast a wistful glance through the steamed up glass, nodding at the little sparrow dining on what sure as hell looked swell, and moved on along the dimly lit walk.

Behind him, one of the waitresses lounging at the counter behind the one customer laughed, "*Ay, que som-*

brero! That one looks like perhaps a matador, no?"

Her companion said, "Who cares? Was most handsome and I bet you that one *es un amante tremendo y que sabe chichar como loco!*"

Phoebe Blake wasn't certain that greaser gal had just said the good looking sport in the funny hat seemed a gent who knew how to fuck like mad. But she knew Lefty had told her to watch out for anything unusual around the hotel across the way, and the good looking sport had just come out of the hotel taproom. Following him surely beat just sitting at a fogged-up chili parlor window. So why not follow him?

Chapter 8

After they'd built the first Crystal Palace in London and a copycat Crystal Palace in New York, it seemed most everybody wanted their own Crystal Palace, albeit the one in Ogallala, like the one down in Tombstone, just said it was a Crystal Palace and had regular walls and the usual pressed-tin ceiling.

But after that, it was bigger than most gaming establishments betwixt the U.P. Depot and the stockyards. So Longarm, gussied up as the flashy Frank Mason who kept saying he was Jones, ambled in to take in such action as they had to offer on a workday eve.

Such action in a cow-town spread like the Crystal Palace tended to be more modest in numbers and serious in intent on a workday eve, with the working stiffs packing it in for the night by nine or so. Those still up and about tended to be ladies of the evening and gentlemen of leisure, if they were interested in said ladies, or sporting gents, if they were more interested in the gentlemen of leisure. The whores and gamblers preyed on the big spending railroad and cattle barons on about a ten-to-one ratio, with one rich asshole supporting a mixed bag of whores, pimps, gamblers and ass kissers hanging about for crumbs. He knew the pack stalking each big spender guarded their intended prey as a pride of lions guard the limping zebra they've laid claim to and so, having already walked away from one fight earlier, Longarm bellied up to the bar, ordered a highball to nurse, and stayed put for a spell with his back to the bar but one boot heel hooked over the brass rail along the base of the same as he took in the crowd, and vice versa.

They sent a painted B girl in a low-cut cancan outfit in to size him up first. She said they called her Bulgarian Billie because that was the way she liked it and added she was surely thirsty.

Longarm nodded pleasantly and said, "I'd be Frank Jones, and I'm with it, Miss Billie."

She frowned and demanded, "With what? You don't work here! I know all the hairpins who work this side of town and you ain't one of them."

Longarm replied, "Working for my ownself. When I said I was with it I meant I was . . . let's call it educated. But the evening is so young and you're so beautiful, I feel sure some sport will slake your thirst for tea water at bourbon prices, ere long."

Bulgarian Billie laughed mockingly and declared, "I'll have you know, sir, nobody buys this girl a lousy shot of *whiskey!* It's four star brandy, in a dollar snifter, if you want to hear my sad story of a fallen angel brought up by honest but overly strict parents."

Longarm nodded soberly and replied, "I once was an honest young cowhand, engaged to a minister's daughter, but then this traveling show came through and I throwed it all away to run off with a snake-charming gal old enough to be ashamed of herself, had she known what it was to feel shame."

Bulgarian Billie shook her head wearily and said, "They were right. You're as carny as you dress for the evening. But be advised all the corners this side of the stockyards have been claimed. Set up a shell game or a faro shoe this side of the colored quarter and there's just no telling what might happen to a pilgrim with no protection, if you know what I mean."

He said, "I know what you mean. I might buy a lady a drink if she was able to tell me who I see about protection in this neck of the woods. I just got in from Denver and . . ."

"They told me how you left Denver in a hurry, Mr. Mason," she cut in with a toss of her head. "Wasn't sure it was you until I had a chance to size up the tailored grips on that six-gun you wear cross-draw under that sissy-looking frock coat. You don't have to buy me nothing. I kind of like your style and, seeing we seem cut from the same cloth, I'll tell you not to ask anyone else how you ask for protection in this town. Asking such questions can take fifty years off a man's life in this town, see?"

He nodded soberly and replied, "I follow your drift, and I like *your* style, too, Bulgarian Billie. So I reckon I'll just wait and see if I get the cold shoulder or a helping hand, here in Ogallala. I got enough to tide me over a few days without stepping on no toes. If nobody asks me to stay by the time I'm running low, I'll just have to get it on down the road and, in either case, it's been an honor meeting up with another well-brung-up child gone wrong."

She laughed, called him a sort of sweet goof for a man who knew his way around, and crawfished back into the milling crowd and tobacco haze to no doubt repeat their conversation to the ones who'd sent her. He didn't strain to follow her trim figure and sassy, sky-blue skirts until they just weren't there. He'd already figured she, and whoever she was scouting for, would want to talk him over on the sly.

As Frank Mason, Longarm lounged there for the time

it took to while away another highball and two more claros. It got tedious as hell.

By this time, the games still going had gotten tight and
serious with nobody on the premises young or drunk
enough to crow or bitch as they won or lost. From what
Longarm could see of the nearest poker game, he being
pretty good at poker himself, a beefy, smooth-shaven old
fart, dressed for riding, albeit expensively, as Buffalo Bill,
had lost a pile already and kept raising. Either he was
dumb as hell or awesomely rich. Longarm knew, as the
cattle baron knew, a man with really deep pockets had to
come out ahead, sooner or later, in an honest poker game.

When a man had the jingle to just keep raising, no
matter what cards he held, he soon had all the other honest
players on the ropes, forced to throw more and more into
the pot no matter how good the hands they held might
strike them. Past a certain point, it was safe to assume a
man raising another hundred or so was either a long lost
Vanderbilt or capable of showing a royal flush anytime
he needed one. The well-heeled stockman struck Longarm
as stinking rich. So the lean and mean-looking cuss in the
planter's hat, who kept calling and raising, had to be a
mechanic who liked to live dangerously.

The beefy cattle baron was not alone in the Crystal
Palace that night. It was safe to assume a beef tycoon who
took such good care of himself paid better than the going
rates to his help. So the half dozen younger riders in almost matching, black, tailored charro outfits, top of the
line black Stetsons and identical Schofield .45s were interested in the game as well, judging from the way they
just stood there watching, like well-trained hawks waiting
on orders to stir a feather.

Longarm had long since learned that when trouble was
brewing and a man didn't have a chip in the game to be
won or lost, he was a total asshole to stay for the party.
So, seeing they hadn't sent him all that way to bear wit-

ness at a coroner's hearing, Longarm set his glass on the zinc bar top and headed for the door at an unhurried, but far from pokey pace, not looking back, but keeping an eye on the back bar's big mirror until he was back outside in the bitter gloom. Such street lamps as they had didn't do much for the shaded boardwalks and such window light as there was wasn't much by that hour on a workday eve.

Longarm might have headed either way, it being too cold to just stand there, if a gruff voice hadn't rasped, "I want a word with you, Frank Mason!"

Longarm turned casually, figuring few gents out to backshoot a man on a dark walk called his name ahead of time. The shorter and thinner figure who'd followed him out of the Crystal Palace was sporting a tin star on his sheepskin jacket. Moving in so's Longarm could make out a fairly young rat-face, the local announced, "I'd be County Deputy Jeb Folsom, and we don't want your kind in Keith County, Frank Mason."

Longarm mildly asked, "What kind do you want in Keith County, then?"

Folsom snapped, "Don't get sassy with me, tinhorn! You know what you are and what we thought of your breed when you signed a false name at the Ogallala Overland Rest! We know all about that man you shot over in Denver last week!"

"You got a warrant with any name I'm currently using on it, kid?" the more experienced lawman posing as a bad man dryly asked.

Folsom said, "Don't push your luck with this child, you fancy dan with the double-action .44! I've a mind to issue you an invite to a leather slapping contest, here and now, since you're supposed to be so good with that gun."

"Don't," said Longarm, flatly. He was aware others had stopped to listen in as he calmly continued, "I don't know what Santa Claus said when he put that badge in your

73

stocking, kid. But Ned Buntline's *Wild West* magazine notwithstanding, nobody, repeat *nobody*, is allowed to up and draw on another man without just cause."

Raising his voice to be heard farther out in the gloom, Longarm went on, "You have no warrant on me. I ain't done anything you can arrest me for. So do you draw on me, I won't be resisting arrest. I'll be shooting a total asshole in self-defense."

Somebody laughed. Longarm wanted to kiss whoever it was.

The blustering county man tried, "I never said I was arresting you. I said we had no use for your kind in Keith County, Mason. So if you know what's good for you, you'll be leaving, east or west, aboard the next train through. Makes no never mind to me. Just so we understand one another."

Longarm said, "I understand you all too well, you yellow dog turd with a badge you don't deserve!"

Folsom gasped, "See here, I'll have you know . . ."

"I know why you're out here rawhiding a stranger in town when it's your *duty* to keep the peace in this here town tonight. That's why they call you a peace officer, see?"

The younger lawman stammered, "I reckon I know I'm a peace officer and right now you're disturbing the hell out of the peace in these parts, Frank Mason!"

Longarm said, "No, I ain't. Until you just now stuck your nose in my beeswax, I was alone on this walk, not bothering a soul. You chose to disturb my peace because, like myself, you sensed trouble brewing back in the Crystal Palace and didn't have the grit to stay put there and keep the peace, like you're supposed to."

Folsom tried, "Saloon brawls ain't county matters. We were talking about my running you out of Keith County, remember?"

Longarm said, "I'll remember and so will the opposition newspapers in this election year, if you'd care to run me in now. To run me in you got to write me up and, once you do, the cub reporters they put to reading the police blotters are going to ask your boss, the sheriff, if they can interview such a notorious mystery man as me. How do you like it so far?"

Folsom tried, "I don't know what you're talking about."

Longarm said, loud enough for all to hear and hopefully repeat, "Sure you do. When all those reporters ask me how come you ran me in with no charges that stuck, I'll be proud to tell them you thought it safer to mess with a man doing nothing on the street than to mess with that tense situation in the Crystal Palace, going on right now, even as we speak!"

Someone else said, "By damn, the stranger's right. Duke Roberts and his boys did ride in this afternoon with the announced intention of a go-for-broke draw poker session with Diamond Donald Dillon!"

Another mildly observed, "Ain't the Roberts's spread well out of town on range patrolled as a rule by the Sheriff's Department, speaking of election years?"

Deputy Folsom sniffed, "Aw, shove it up all your asses! I got better things to do than argue with a bunch of fucking drunks!"

As he stormed away, yet another voice declared, "You got sand in your craw, stranger. You say they call you Mason?"

Longarm shrugged and said, "*He* did. I disremember what name I might be traveling under, this evening."

Then he strode off, fast, as, behind him, a townee murmured, "I hear-tell he shot a man in Denver and *they* were afraid to mess with him, too!"

Longarm tried not to grin like a mean little kid. You never knew who was watching in such tricky light. He walked right past Phoebe Blake as she huddled out of the wind in the entrance of a dark and shutdown hat shop.

She'd heard the whole exchange, of course. She followed the handsome brute just far enough to see he was headed back to his own hotel, as if to be off the streets of Ogallala when that trouble he'd just made mention of cut loose.

Phoebe headed for her own hotel, not wanting to be rounded up as a possible witness, either. She found Lefty jawing with Oregon Bob upstairs, seeing nobody could fornicate with Verona all the time.

As she joined them, helping herself to a stiff jolt to recover from the cold outside, Lefty asked what she'd found out, over by the late Longarm's hotel.

Phoebe said, "Things over yonder have cooled off. The gal Longarm had shacked up with is long gone. Likely back to Denver with his body. They rented his room to somebody else you might be interested in, Lefty."

"Another lawman?" the would-be bank robber asked in a worried tone.

Phoebe poured herself another drink as she dimpled and said, "Not hardly. His name's Frank Mason. He seems to be walking, not running, away from a shooting in other parts. To look at him, you might take him for a color blind dapper dan. They say he has an eye for the ladies and you can smell his bay rum from pistol range. But he's tougher than he looks. Tough enough to stand up to a county lawman, just now, and send him packing with his tail between his legs."

Lefty frowned thoughtfully to ask, "You suppose he could be out to rob somebody here in Ogallala before *we* can get around to 'em, Phoebe?"

The innocent looking but bitter little thing suggested, "Why don't we ask him? From all I've been able to gather, he lit out alone after that shooting. So he ain't hooked up with any other *men* here in this town."

Lefty glanced at Oregon Bob, who nodded and said,

"We surely need the extra help, if this big bad wolf is looking for a job."

Lefty turned to Phoebe to ask, "You reckon you could get . . . closer to this Frank Mason and sound him out for us, sweet stuff?"

Phoebe smiled like Mona Lisa coming up with something really dirty as she purred, "Be my pleasure and I'm sort of looking forward to it."

Chapter 9

Longarm knew the shape-shifting Salome Morrigan was waiting for him up in 3-E, but he was getting his second wind as the hands of that Regulator brand clock above the taproom bar stood close to ten P.M. So he bellied up to the bar, ordered a beer and waited for a lull in the game in the corner before he announced, loud enough to be clearly heard, "Speaking in a fatherly tone, I advise one and all of you gents to stay put, regardless of the hands you may hold at the moment. For we'll all want to be able to say we were here in this respectable taproom, acting sedate, when that shoot-out at the Crystal Palace broke out."

He let that sink in as he sipped some suds, then added, "So none of us know shit about it, and Doc, here, can swear to our pure collective innocence."

The dealer with his back to the corner, Spats Gordon, stared hard through the tobacco haze for a time before he called back, "Much obliged. Couple of the boys were fixing to call it a night. But you say there's trouble at the Palace? What sort of trouble, Mr. . . . Jones?"

Longarm said, "Cards. An immovable dealer versus an irresistible player who is backing his bets with deep pockets and half a dozen gun hands. You all might be better off if I left you sort of fuzzy as to details, lest you sound too smart when you tell the law you don't know nothing about such distant rumbles."

One of the players bucking Spats sighed and said, "I heard-tell Duke Roberts was riding in for a showdown with Diamond Donald most any night now! They say old Duke heard-tell how Diamond Donald laughed at him and said he was a born sucker!"

Segundo Stan soberly demanded, "What else would you call a man who cuts cards, winner-take-all, with a professional gambler?"

Someone else observed, "Just the same, it was dumb of Diamond Donald to crow about it around town. Old Duke's a sore loser with a temper and some weight to throw around. So why don't you deal some more, Spats?"

As the corner game proceeded, Doc leaned over the bar to say, "Thanks, Mr. Jones."

Longarm shrugged and replied, "May as well call me Mason, seeing the local law in the person of a pimple-faced deputy named Folsom chooses to so-describe this child. It's none of my never mind what the management may or may not own in yonder corner. But didn't you say that game goes on here most every night?"

When Doc hesitated, Longarm said, "I've a reason for asking."

Doc shrugged and said, "Every night but the Sabbath, with the usual, ah, tip to the barkeep. What was your reason for asking?"

Longarm said, "By now you have some inkling as to who I might be and a county deputy was just speculating on what I might be doing here. So I'll tell you true, I've been hoping to meet up with an old pal who's been known to frequent this end of the Ogallala Trail."

He sipped more suds and continued, "I disremember the name he may be using, current. He's a tall, lean breed with a hatchet face under a slate gray ten-gallon. Wears his own .44-40 lower than mine in a side-draw tied-down rig and, just remembered, he laces his suds with *rum*, like he thinks he's a fucking pirate!"

There was no such person, of course. Longarm had just whipped his sinister sounding pal up by describing Deputy Smiley back in Denver and then throwing in an unlikely drink a barkeep would feel sure he'd remember serving.

It worked. Doc shook his head and said, "Nope. Only other transient we've served recent, aside from yourself and that lawman who got shot in here the other night, was a short, stubby Eastern dude who insulted me by asking if I could fix him up with a gal who gave French lessons. He said he'd read in this travel book how wild and wooly the gals were, out our way. Ain't that a bitch?"

Longarm said, "Every well-traveled man knows it's the bellhops you ask for that sort of service in a transient hotel. I heard about that lawman getting shot in here. Was he here at the bar or playing cards in the corner with the boys that night?"

Doc said, "Just to the left of where you're standing at this very bar. The game hadn't started yet, thank God. For I hate to think what a mess we'd have had to clean up had he been seated at yonder table of a Saturday night!"

Longarm grimaced at the picture and casually asked, "This Longarm was a sporting man as well as a lawman, then?"

Doc shrugged and confided, "He should have stuck to being a famous lawman. He didn't know how to buck blackjack worth shit. He had deep pockets, for an honest lawman. So he wagered like a college boy know-it-all with a wonderous system he'd just dreamed up!"

Longarm nodded knowingly and asked, "You don't mean he'd invented the foolproof system of doubling his next bet?"

Doc laughed disdainfully and replied, "Foolproof in theory. Not in practice. The notion that when you lose one you should bet two with even odds you'll win your lost money back falls apart as soon as you know the odds are always with the dealer and that doubling your wager gets astronomical after you've doubled it two, four, eight, sixteen and so on 'til there ain't that much money on Earth!"

Longarm shrugged and decided, "You're right. He should have stuck with games he knew. Have you heard any more about his murder?"

Doc said, "Not recent. Hear his body was shipped home in a lead-lined coffin, under a cloud. Town lawman who drops by for the free lunch now and again says it 'peers a once-famous federal lawman may have taken to drinking and gambling unwisely of late. Seems he had no call to be over in these parts and nobody had ever asked him to investigate trail brands outside the jurisdiction of his home office."

Longarm nodded soberly and declared, "Drinking and gambling and wild, wild women have been the ruination of many a man on either side of the law. Heard mention of him demanding bond money. They patted his body down as he lay there in the sawdust, I assumes?"

Doc sighed and said, "The town law, then the county law, then some federal deputies from Marshal Fender's outfit, of course. The federal crew seemed to suspect the local badges might be holding out on them. The fucking sheriff as much as accused this child of robbing the dead before I called the law. But you can ask the lobby crew next door if I had the chance! They all come running when that greaser flopped dead in that archway leading out to the lobby!"

Longarm smiled thinly and said, "I just tangled with a suspicious county badge called Folsom. I can hardly wait for him to come busting in here, any minute, to ask us what we know about the trouble down the way at the Crystal Palace!"

But as the corner game went on and Longarm swilled more suds than any man with a willing woman waiting had any call to swill, nobody came busting in out of the silent night. And as it kept getting later, the night outside got silent as midnights tend to on a work-night eve in a town the size of Ogallala.

As a distant clock struck twelve, Doc rang for the night bellhop on duty in the lobby next door and bet him four bits he couldn't run down to the Palace and find out why things were so slow.

By this time, Spats Gordon, being prudent as well as clannish, folded the house game in the far corner, standing everyone in the joint, winners, losers and even pains in the ass in purple hats, to their pleasures at the bar. So Longarm found himself included as the regulars bellied up to either side of him. Of course, that had been the way he'd hoped things might go.

Save for his face-saving remark about purple hats, the tinhorn who held court there most nights seemed to include "Mr. Jones, Mr. Mason or Whatever-the-fuck-your-name-might-be" in the hilarity when the bellhop returned to report the results of that other game down the way.

According to the bellhop, they'd still been laughing, over to the Crytal Palace, after the imperious Duke Roberts and his boys had left, shortly after Diamond Donald had crawled.

The way the bellhop had heard it, things had built to a breathless climax by the time Diamond Donald had modestly allowed he had a full house. But before he'd been able to rake in the considerable pot, old Duke had said, "Hold on there, pilgrim. For your winning streak just ended, and I declare myself the winner."

When Diamond Donald had asked to see the hand that beat a full house, old Duke Roberts had spread two pair and a Schofield .45 with five in the wheel out in front of him to quietly ask if that didn't have any fucking full house dealt by a cocksucker beat.

To which Diamond Donald had, of course, replied, "It surely does, Mr. Roberts! How come you're so lucky tonight?"

When the sports in the Ogallala Overland Rest's taproom finished laughing, Spats Gordon winked at Ace Perdue to warn, "Let that be a lesson to us all, Ace. Never win big off the same mark night after night and, above all, never *laugh* at him when he's got what amounts to a squad of dragoons on his payroll!"

Segundo Stan said, "Them D Bar D riders *practice* with them fancy Schofields, too. One of *my* riders seen 'em shooting cans off fence posts *blam-blam-blam* like they were getting their costly army rounds free, off the army!"

Another regular dressed cow said, "Old Duke gets a price by buying ammunition in bulk, same as the army you just mentioned. Most old boys are content with the same ammo in cheaper Colt '74 Peacemakers. When a man arms all his riders with six-guns serious as them long-barreled and quicker loading Schofields, he's not a man you want to laugh at!"

Having agreed Diamond Donald had shown some common sense for a change, and having more than one woman waiting up they were going to have to explain the story to, the gathering began to break up.

As Longarm thanked Spats Gordon for that nightcap and headed for the archway, Spats called him aside to murmur in a desperately casual way, "I hope it's understood I only meant to test a new kid in the school yard, earlier. Is it understood we ain't, ah, *worried* about nothing?"

Longarm said, "Let's say you ain't afraid of me and I ain't afraid of you and let's agree it makes more sense for wolves to hunt sheep than one another. I'd shake on that if the last man who tried that in this joint had survived the experiment!"

They both laughed and parted friendly in the archway. Things were turning out swell, considering this had been his first night in a new town. Longarm knew that to the regulars in this neck of Ogallala, he'd still be the new kid in the school yard for a spell. But to anybody else who came along, he might pass for one of the regulars, and a regular to be treated with respect because he didn't take much shit and some said he'd shot a man, somewhere, sometime.

Longarm moved up the back stairs, checked the match stem under his own door to make sure he hadn't had any recent visitors, and went on up to Room 3-E to find Salome Morrigan pacing the rug in her mules and kimono with her hair let down, waving an angry French cigarette in a fancy holder at him like a baton as she demanded to know who he'd been with all this time.

Longarm bolted her door behind him and hung his fancy Spanish hat on the knob as he turned, peeling off his lavender frock coat to tell her, "I have spent the evening in the company of ugly men and that has given me a hard-on you'll never forgive me for!"

She laughed despite herself as he unbuckled his gun rig, advancing to kiss her as he hung his .44-40 handy on the head post.

Having such a head start at undressing, she naturally beat him into the bed, and damned if she hadn't shifted her shape some more as she presented her perky rump dog style with an arch glance over her shoulder, saying, "I want to talk while we fuck, darling."

Longarm allowed he was game for any position that didn't hurt as he quickly shed what was left. He felt no call to mention he'd noticed in the past, with other ladies, dog style was the most conversational if less romantic position.

As he stepped up to the plate bare-assed to take a hip bone in each hand and let it find its own way home, he never asked what she wanted to talk about. He knew what she'd been pacing the rug over.

She felt between her thighs to take the matter in hand and guide him in, hissing in mingled surprise and pleasure, "Don't ask me how, but I'd forgotten how grand that feels, this way. Move it all you care to, lover, but while you're at it . . . what if Price left a money belt in your room, meaning to come back for it after he and his doxie were all squared away to skedaddle and then, when he got shot downstairs . . ."

Longarm thrust in and out as the lady had requested, assuring her, "He'd never do that. All the ways the two of us have guessed at add up awkward. They were fixing to make a run for it. Knowing more than one of the men he was running from might pat him down, unexpected, he gave the bulk of what they had betwixt them to Zilphia La Belle, like she said. So when he got shot, she ran for it, alone, and the rest we know."

Salome gasped, "Could you move it left and right as you shove it in and out? That's why they call it screwing. . . . That feels grand. Zilphia La Belle didn't have half the money he had shaken those stockmen down for with worthless receipts when the Pinks caught up with her!"

Longarm insisted, "She had all the getaway money they had left to get away with. Nobody hid any away in this hotel. Nobody robbed a famous dead man in front of all them witnesses. Ain't you figured it out, yet?"

To which she demurely replied, "No. Let me get on top so I can screw it in and out *right* while you *tell* me, lover!"

Chapter 10

Like her fairy namesake, Salome Morrigan was able to shift her swell shape to look like a whole new nude as they changed positions. Gripping the head rail of the hired bed as she planted a bare heel to either side of Longarm's naked hips to screw up and down his inspired erection in a whole new way, she demanded, "So where is the money, honey? That Zilphia La Belle had less than half what he'd stung those stockmen for. So if he didn't have it on him, and nobody stole it from one or the other, where could it have gone?"

Speaking mighty calmly for a man about to come, Longarm told Salome, "He piddled it all away, of course. The two of them were living high, and I just learned downstairs he thought he knew how to play cards. I reckon his mamma never warned him about friendly little blackjack games where the deal don't change with every hand. For a con man, the late Parson Price knew nothing about card sharks and . . . Hold on a second!"

She dimpled down at him to say, "Why thank you and was all that meant for little me? You come like a schoolboy in a cathouse, bless your horny heart and . . . Oh, Jeeeepers! Me, too!"

They were at it with the lamp shedding soft romantic light on their love-slicked writhings. So as Oregon Bob joined Phoebe Blake across the way, the mousy little brunette was staring wistfully up at the shadow show on Salome's window shade.

Oregon Bob said, "I just missed him at the taproom across the street. Same barkeep never recognized me in these duds with my lip shaved and my hair blacker than your own right now. Doc says your tough old Frank Mason and the boys he was drinking with just called it a night. I was too slick to ask at the desk if he'd gone upstairs."

Phoebe said, "He's gone upstairs. This would be a bad time to call on him, Bob."

Oregon Bob followed her gaze to the one third-story, lamplit window, stared just long enough to figure out what he was looking at and decided, "He's got a gal up yonder. A shapely one. On top. And look at her go!"

Phoebe sniffed, "You should have seen him throwing it to her dog style a while back. He sure moves swell, and he dosen't seem to need any rest between times, neither!"

Oregon Bob laughed and said, "Lefty never sent us over here to see how fine he fucks. The question before the house is whether he is or is he not a rider of the owlhoot trail."

Phoebe said, "That sheriff's deputy seemed to think so. Some others I overheard made mention of some shootings and lawmen afraid to serve him with a warrant. You should have been there earlier, Bob. He as much as dared that deputy to draw, in front of witnesses!"

Oregon Bob said, "It's established he's mean. But we got no use for *crazy* mean! We need to recruit at least two cool hard cases to help us with that bank withdrawal Lefty's working out, now that Longarm tipped that first bank off. Do you reckon you could, ah, get yourself into that same position with him and mayhaps find out whether he screws like a natural man or goes crazy when he's excited?"

Phoebe made a wry face and sniffed, "It makes a girl feel so fine to have her pussy towed like a target past possible maniacs!"

Watching the shifting shapes against the window shade across the way, she laughed bitterly and said, "I reckon I'd be willing to take such a chance, if that particular maniac wasn't already fucking someboy else like, well, a maniac."

Oregon Bob laughed and said, "Neither one of us are going to get anything but hard feelings and head colds out here in the dark, Phoebe. What say we head back to our own hotel and you can suck my poor frozen dick before it drops off."

She started to say something dumb. It was dumb to say things that made men hit you. And a girl with murder warrants out on her and no other skills but screwing and sneaking had no other men to turn to. So she heaved a defeated sigh and said, "I guess. But if I give you a French lesson will you strum my old banjo, at least, so's I can get a good night's sleep for a change?"

Oregon Bob replied, expansively, "Hell, honey, get it really hard for me and I might even favor you with a fuck!"

"You're all so good to me," the little sparrow murmured as she followed him off into the bitter darkness.

Back upstairs, Salome Morrigan was commencing to pout, now that she'd come more than once and "Frank Mason" kept insisting she was full of shit about all that missing money.

Knowing how women talked, and seeing others had commented on his sharing a three-for-a-nickel cheroot with them afterwards, Longarm was dying for a smoke but was not rude enough to light a claro in the company of a lady he dared not offer a drag. So he could only run a strand of her straw-colored hair through his teeth like, well, a straw, as she finally decided, "I fear you're right, Frank. A lawman gone wrong, or a gentleman of the road pretending to be one, wouldn't likely invest his ill-gotten gains in stock futures or secured bonds. So the damned fool blew more than half of the money he swindled on women, whiskey and wagers and those men who killed him were probably working for some big cattleman he'd swindled, right?"

Longarm said, "I like that notion as well as any other." And this was the simple truth when he studied on it.

Salome said, "At least the two of us met here at last. So my run over from Omaha wasn't totally wasted. You are coming back to Omaha with me now, aren't you?"

Longarm answered without taking time to study on it, "Why would I want to go to Omaha?"

He'd already figured what he *should* have said before she sat bolt upright with the lamplight glistening on her naked charms to glare down at him and hiss, "Why . . . you . . . bastard! Is that all I was to you, a fast, free lay in a second-class cow town hotel?"

He reached out a hand to circle her bare behind as he soothed, "I meant why would I go to such a big town with such a big police force and Lord knows how many warrants out on me? *You're* the one who just now said she wants to break this up, after using and abusing me like your India rubber toy!"

She had to laugh. She slapped at him, called him a big fibber and when he tried to pull her back down, she pulled away and said he wasn't fooling her for one minute.

Longarm insisted, "Did anyone around this child hear him say he wanted to leave his present company? Didn't I come back here, pure and horny as ever, after a night on a cowtown where wild, wild women are hanging from the rafters? I passed on a pretty little brunette who was lusting after me out a chili parlor window, earlier. Then, I passed on a dance hall gal they call Bulgarian Billie because she likes it Bulgarian style and you know where the English troops picked up the notion of buggery, serving in the Balkans with Bulgarian dragoons."

Salome stopped struggling but remained upright as she sniffed, "I'm touched. You came back to a sure thing and now it's just tough titty if I have to go back to Omaha alone?"

Longarm said, "I ain't asking you to go nowheres. I got to stay here in Ogallala because I'm hoping to meet up with an old pal who drives cows up the Ogallala Trail from Texas every year about this time. I mean, I'm waiting *serious*, honey."

She let him pull her back down as she asked, "What are the two of you planning to steal, then?"

Knowing she was a bounty huntress when she wasn't on top, Longarm told her, "I ain't out to rob nobody. I want to get put in touch with somebody who can get me off in case this little misunderstanding I had back in Colorado goes sour on me."

As he snuggled her closer, he explained, "This old boy I shot just in fun said he won't press charges, seeing I only shot him once and paid good money to have the bleeding stopped in time. But you know how it is with bullet wounds."

She murmured, "No, I don't. I've never been shot, knock wood, and what do you think you're doing to my ring dang doo, you naughty boy?"

He answered, "Can't you tell? Just open wide and say, *ah*, whilst I explain about mortified wounds. No more than half the old boys who get shot die right then and there on the spot. But more than half the ones only wounded up and die days or weeks later from gangrene and such. So whilst I'm waiting to see if I'm in the clear, I mean to find me a big shot with the ways and means to get me off no matter what."

She languidly replied, "You mean a fixer. I know some fixers back in Omaha, but fix me up with another sweet screwing and we'll talk about it later!"

So he did, but they didn't, or, at least, "Frank Mason" refused to consider anyone in Omaha trying to fix a shooting in Denver, because Longarm knew Judge Dickerson wanted him to find out who that fucking fixer in *Leavenworth* was. There were only so many days in a year with so many ducks to shoot.

In the end, having most likely screwed to the point of showing off her ownself, Salome was a good sport about letting Frank Mason off with buying her a hearty breakfast downstairs and walking her and her baggage to the U.P. Depot in the warmer sunlight of a more seasonable October morning on the Great Plains.

Salome's eastbound passed through around ten A.M., so they had plenty of time to kill, even after a morning quickie and a more wistful shower together with the public bathroom door locked, as she giggled some.

So whilst neither noticed, they were tailed to the depot, as Lefty ordered another breakfast, with Phoebe Blake tagging catty corner whilst Oregon Bob strolled half a block behind them, acting as if he didn't know anyone on either side of the busy street.

Given his practice with railroad timetables, Longarm got Salome to the depot early enough to swap some spit with her on the platform.

Neither Phoebe nor Oregon Bob were inexperienced enough to go out on the platform after them and the others about to board. There was a long snack counter along one wall of the waiting room inside. So Phoebe took a seat near the middle whilst Oregon Bob ordered his own coffee and donuts from a stool at the far end. They'd agreed as they split up in the entrance that they'd wait for Frank

Mason to either board the train or head back into town before they moved. They had agreed that Mason leaving town with that fancy gal meant Lefty had no further call to think about him. On the other hand, if he saw the gal off and went back to his hotel, Bob could see about striking up a conversation with him in that taproom.

All bets were off, of course, if he headed for the Western Union or any of the banks in town. Lefty hadn't cottoned to the notion of Frank Mason moving into Longarm's room no matter what some said about that trouble he was in.

Out on the platform, Salome had pressed her business card with her Omaha address on Frank Mason, and Longarm sincerely meant to look her up the next time he passed through Omaha, with a view to enjoying a good laugh with a swell lay in such an otherwise dull railroad terminal.

While all this was going on, the armed and dangerous Duke Roberts was driving toward the U.P. Depot with his six men, all armed and dangerous, tagging after him on their horses.

The cattle baron wasn't after anybody that morning. He was in a fairly good mood, for Duke Roberts. The night before, he'd made a monkey out of that tinhorn who'd laughed behind his back, and now he was fixing to meet the young widow of an old pal, who was arriving from the East at his invite with her two young boys so's their "Uncle Duke" could show 'em how to rope and throw like real cowboys instead of sissy kids.

They'd arrive with their pretty young mother, Miss Una Clarke née MacAlpin, shortly after that infernal ten A.M. eastbound cleared the tracks by passing Miss Una's siding at Roscoe. The damned U.P. would have double tracks all the way out to Ogden had Duke Roberts been in charge.

Before he and his boys could get there, the eastbound holding things up for Roberts arrived. So Longarm put

Salome and her two bags on board and bet the porter a silver dollar he couldn't see the lady to a window seat in a no smoking car.

She was crying as she turned away. Longarm muttered, "Aw, mush," and headed back inside.

In spite of his earlier breakfast, or mayhaps because of the way old Salome had stared at him when he'd suggested steak with their eggs, he still felt a tad empty. So seeing he had nothing more important at the moment to worry about, he moseyed over, took a seat down at one end from from the smooth-shaven rider dunking donuts at the far end and told the motherly counter lady he'd like a cup of joe and mayhaps half a dozen donuts his ownself. The one other patron at that hour was a little old sparrow gal in a veiled black hat with a hard-to-decide-on cloth coat. It looked sort of gray or sort of blue or sort of rusty, depending on how the light hit it. The little gal seemed flustered by his staring at her coat. Longarm ticked the brim of his Spanish hat to her and looked away, lest she take him for a moon calf flirting with a school marm or mayhaps a cleaning woman in a public place, for Gawd's sake.

Then, just as Longarm was served his heroic order by the bemused old counter lady, a big, gray bear proceeded by half a dozen smaller black panthers swaggered up to the counter.

Looking neither to his right nor left, the black clad rider who got there first told the little sparrow gal, "Move your skinny ass either way along the counter so's the seven of us can set, sis!"

Phoebe Blake rose to her feet as if she'd been pinched on the bottom. So did Longarm, a lot higher, to drift their way with a thin smile as he gently but firmly declared, "You are way out of line, cowboy. That ain't no way to talk to a lady, and so now I reckon you want to tell this lady you are sincerely sorry, don't you?"

The younger gunslick stared at Longarm thunder-ghasted as all six of the others circled in, like surprised wolves.

The one Longarm had challenged asked, "Have you been drinking? Don't you know who I work for, pilgrim?"

To which Longarm, could only reply, "Don't want to know. Don't care. You have just insulted this lady, serious, and now you are fixing to apologize or slap leather. It's no never mind to me, either way."

Chapter 11

It got mighty quiet in the U.P. waiting room as Longarm waited to see what happened next, managing by sheer willpower not to let his tense tingles show.

A million years went by and then another member of the pack quietly asked, "Boss?"

Duke Roberts said, "I'm still studying. I'm afraid I wasn't paying attention to the onset of this situation. Did you just cuss that lady, Alamo?"

Alamo Jack Aherne stammered, "I just asked her nice to make room for you, boss."

The imperious older man fixed Longarm with one bright blue eye half shut and the other beaming like a locomotive headlight at him as he asked, "What can I tell you, mister? Whether he's in the right or in the wrong, he rides for me and there's seven of us and one of you."

Longarm said, "I noticed," as he shot a disgusted glance at the other male customer seated at the far end. Then he asked the cattle baron, "What can I tell *you*? A gentleman who don't call a coward who'd cuss a woman ain't no gentleman and we all got to die *some* day. If I can't take you all with me, I can try to take some and like the dog soldiers say, this is as good a day to die as any other. So what's it going to be?"

Duke Roberts laughed and said, "By jimmies, I think he means it! You better tell his sweetheart you're sorry, Alamo!"

Alamo Jack paled and protested, "Are we gonna let this dude in a lavender coat back the D Bar D down, boss?"

Duke Roberts said, "The D Bar D never cussed no lady and you don't work for it no more, Alamo. You hired on to fight for me, not for me to fight at times and places of your own choosing."

Then he swept ten gallons worth of Stetson from his white head to bow with a flourish to Phoebe Blake as he added, "Your servant, ma'am, and I hope you understand this beef is not betwixt the D Bar D and you two sweethearts."

"He's not my sweetheart, and I never asked nobody to fight over me!" the little sparrow flustered, blushing like a rose behind her veil.

The bluff stockman shot Longarm a startled look, shrugged, and told Alamo Jack, "You're up against a gallant sap or a homicidal lunatic and either way you are purely on your own. So it's time to fight, it's time to run, or it's time to tell the lady you're sorry, old son!"

Alamo flushed beet red and couldn't meet Phoebe's eye as he managed to stammer, "I didn't mean nothing disrespectsome, lady. I was only out to make way for my boss and if I used any dirty words I disremember, I am sincerely sorry and I ask you to forgive me."

The flustered little sparrow managed to reply, "Of course. Oh dear, I think I'm fixing to cry!"

Then she turned away to move down to the far end of the counter and bury her face in the shirt of the grown man who hadn't lifted a finger in her defense. Longarm was only mildly surprised. He'd long since known that if he lived to be a hundred, he'd never understand women and their wondrous ways.

Duke Roberts asked Longarm if the war was over. Longarm nodded at Alamo Jack thoughtfully and replied, "Far as I'm concerned, and by now, my coffee is getting cold. So why don't we all just dunk our donuts and say no more about it?"

Duke Roberts took the stool next to Longarm and as the others started to follow suit, the stockman they'd all hired on with quietly but firmly said, "It's still a free country, Alamo. But if you mean to order, I want you to know you'll be paying out of your own pocket because, like I said, you don't work for me no more."

Alamo protested, "Aw, come on, I was only trying to make way for *you*, boss!"

But Duke Roberts insisted, "I ain't your boss no more. A man who asks his boss to back his play when he's out of line ain't worth . . . spit, on account there's ladies present. Like I said, it's still a free country. But if I were you, I'd ride out to the D Bar D ahead of everybody, pack my gear and leave an address with the cook so's we can mail your pay at the end of the month."

Alamo sniffed, "Aw, boss . . ." and started to sit down. But then another black clad rider for the D Bar D growled, "Don't. The Duke suggested you ride and your pony's out front, so what are you waiting for?"

Longarm felt too embarrassed for the man he'd just crawfished to watch as Alamo Jack exited the scene. He just washed down that donut with tepid coffee and signaled the motherly counter lady he'd like a second cup. Duke Roberts told her it would be on him. She shook her head, stared tenderly at Longarm and murmured, "No, it's not. It's on the house."

As she turned away, the older stockman chuckled and confided to the flashy stranger who'd just gotten one of his riders fired, "You sure have a way with the ladies.

How come you don't aim at ladies a mite younger or prettier, mister . . . ?"

"They call me Frank Mason, and I wasn't flirting with nobody just now," Longarm replied. He polished off the last of that cup and went on. "You're likely right. I must be a gallant sap or a homicidal lunatic, unless a mother who raised me to treat all women with respect counts for something."

Duke Roberts looked away sort of wistful, to reply, "I was brung up by quality folk as well. That's how come I wasn't about to back a lout who'd cuss a woman I didn't have down for a fact as a whore. Or do you stand up for whores as well, Mr. Mason?"

Longarm didn't answer as the counter lady served him his fresh cup with a radiant smile. But as she turned away he confided, "It's been known to happen. I ain't sap enough to take a stand in a parlor house and demand all the customers speak respectsome, but if any woman is in my company, acting in a decent way, I expect other gents to treat her decent in front of me."

Longarm cast a thoughtful eye after the little sparrow and that other cuss-dressed cow as they moved on out together before he added, "What the two of them may or may not do after I ain't looking is up to them, of course. Like you said, it's still a free country."

Duke Roberts followed his drift. He nodded at Oregon Bob's retreating back and jeered, "He knew her. Yet he never said boo when another man insulted her. What do you make of him, Mr. Mason?"

Longarm shrugged, dunked another donut, and decided, "Some might say he had more sense than this child. He's likely explaining right now why he thought it sort of stupid to go up against seven guns just because one of them had referred to her bottom as a donkey in the more biblical sense. They might be married. I've felt dumb as hell, more than once, after stopping a man from abusing a

100

woman in public, only to have her turn on me for abusing her man. But what else can you do, stand there like a big-ass bird and let another man get away with that?"

The older man said, "He did, and like you said, he's likely her man or at least close enough to walk her home or back to work. Are you in the market for a job, Mr. Mason?"

"Not riding as a hired gun for the D Bar D." Longarm replied, since this was the simple truth. Duke Roberts was a jovial bully at best and possibly a bad neighbor to share range with. But Billy Vail hadn't sent anyone this far to investigate range hogging. That was a local matter they elected sheriffs to worry about.

Duke Roberts said, "Study on it. I like your style and, as you surely noticed, I'm missing a hand who knew how to rope and throw, knew how to handle a gun, but didn't know when to keep his swagger in check."

Then he rose from his stool to drop four bits beside the two donuts he hadn't touched, adding, "I got to get out on the platform, speaking of treating ladies with respect. The westbound's bringing a poor young widow and two godsons born to an old pal of mine. She's too proud to take charity. But when I heard she was having it tough back East, I invited my two godsons out our way for the winter and, who knows, mayhaps next summer. I sent 'em some wooly chaps and a pair of Stetsons and Miss Una wrote they've been pestering her about the trip ever since. Do you reckon that makes me a gallant sap, too, ah . . . Frank?"

Longarm said, "Not in my book. You did say you spon-sored 'em for an old pal and I've yet to meet a kid who didn't like to play cowboy."

They shook on it and parted friendly, albeit some of his wolf pack shot him thoughtful glances as they all got up to trail after him.

Longarm finished the rest of his donuts alone at the

counter and when the motherly old counter lady refused to let him pay and allowed she got off at six, he snapped a quarter on the marble counter and strode out to the sunny street without looking back.

It seemed a poor time on a work day to look for more action in any town that size. So, seeing he hadn't got much rest the night before, Longarm headed back to his hotel to see if he might manage forty winks before things picked up again in Ogallala.

Passing the Western Union, he felt tempted, but he knew his home office wasn't about to send any wires addressed to Frank Mason care of Western Union and he knew from having tailed many a suspect that it was when a man felt sure nobody was watching him, somebody was likely watching him.

He had nothing to report, as yet, in any case. Neither Billy Vail nor the judge would care about any of the action he'd seen over this way, so far. Having established himself as a regular in the vicinity of his own hotel, he meant to give that Crystal Palace another shot, after supper. In the meanwhile, he feared it was safer to lie slug-abed, for he hadn't made contact with a soul his home office would be interested in.

Or so he thought. But at the Hotel Custer, three blocks away, Longarm as Frank Mason was the subject of a heated discussion, with Oregon Bob certain he was too loose a cannon to rob banks with.

As Lefty listened by the window, sneaking peeks out through the slits of the jalousies from time to time while he smoked, Oregon Bob continued, "There were seven of 'em, all heeled with their Schofields in tie-down holsters, and this cross-draw dressed like a fucking pimp never batted an eye when he challenged the one who'd told Phoebe to move her ass!"

Phoebe Blake pouted "He was a real gent and not as

102

dumb about gunplay or good manners as some people I could mention!"

Oregon Bob laughed and explained to Lefty by the window and Verona on the bed. "She got called a lady by three men in a row this morning, and it's gone to her head."

From the bed, Verona asked with a languid yawn if any of them had been good looking.

Phoebe said, "Frank Mason may dress like a tinhorn, but I 'spect he knows a thing or two about gunplay and the odds involved. It's true he took a chance for me, a serious chance. But it was a *calculated* chance. He didn't just look away like a sissy when he saw the one who was mean to me was with a bunch of pals. He knew it was a public place and that any real man could see the one who'd been mean to me was in the wrong. He knew that they knew they'd have a lot to answer for if they killed him. He knew that they knew he'd have a good excuse if he killed any of them. So he stood up for me, like a man, and it worked when the older man those others worked for took off his hat and called me a lady, too!"

"Did you come?" asked Verona, sweetly, from across the room.

Oregon Bob snorted, "I 'spect she did and that's my point, Lefty. I could see, just as good as he could, that the asshole dumb enough to cuss a strange woman in public *might* be on his own if push came to shove. But Frank Mason never laid eyes on old Phoebe before and yet he stood up for her, seven to one, as if she was Queen Victoria!"

"It felt nice. Like I *was* a queen, or at least a lady of quality, and you should have seen the way Frank Mason handles himself in a tight spot, Lefty! He was cool as anything and asked that rascal whether he aimed to apologize or draw—in the same tone he might have asked an old maid if she minded him lighting up on a front porch!"

Verona laughed and opined, "Ain't he cute? Our Phoebe has the gushies for her Galahad and likely vice versa!"

Phoebe looked away as she murmured, "He barely seemed to notice me. I fear he'd have acted the same had that rider insulted the older woman behind the counter. I ain't speaking up for him because we're in love, dad blast it! I'm speaking up for him because Bob, there, has it in for Frank Mason for being more of a man than he was this morning!"

Oregon Bob shot back, "Shut your mouth. You're giving me a hard-on! The man's too wild to ride with us, Lefty. I mean, sure, you want a pard who's man enough to back your play in a shoot-out. But do you want a pard who *starts* a shoot-out for no good reason?"

Phoebe pouted, "He *had* good reason, damn you!"

And to her surprise, Verona chimed in from across the way, "You're right, Phoebe. I told you why I'd never fuck Bob, myself, even if Lefty asked me to!"

Lefty laughed and said, "I fear the votes add up to one against Frank Mason, two votes for Frank Mason with me abstaining 'til we know some more about Frank Mason."

Glancing out the window, Lefty took a thoughtful drag on his smoke before he added, "Thanks to Phoebe, here, we know he likes gals and don't seem afraid of many men. Now I want you to sound him out about where he stands as to riding the owlhoot trail for fun and profit. It don't matter what others say about a man with a rep for pushing back. We need to know how he feels about armed robbery."

Oregon Bob snorted, "Nobody said he ever robbed nobody. The way I hear, he's on the dodge after shooting a man in a card game."

Left said, "My point exactly. I recently heard-tell of this mighty mean consumptive gambler, used to be a dentist back East before his lungs went bad. Down Texas way, he killed more than one man just for distracting him as he was dealing. Yet he recently turned a wanted man in to a lawman he plays cards with, and never asked for no reward. So you got to be careful about moody gents who dress flashy and saunter about sort of scary. Before I let him see this face, I want to know a whole lot more about him and, hell, you recruited Giggles and Weedy for us, didn't you?"

Oregon Bob said, "I guess. What about that other unpredictable hard case you just mentioned, Lefty?"

Lefty answered, "Doc Holliday? None of us has to worry about *that* homicidal lunatic. Last I heard, he'd left for that new silver strike out Tombstone way."

Chapter 12

Bright-eyed and bushy-tailed after a full eight hours sleep, a cold shower alone with a rapidly recovering pecker and a warm meal with plenty of joe, Longarm spent enough time in the taproom of his hotel to establish that nobody there wanted to rob a bank with him before he ambled on to the brighter lights of the Crystal Palace.

That blue norther had blown itself east and, aside from the cornhusk aroma of of the autumn breezes blowing in from the west to help out with the horse shit and coal smoke of a town that size, it felt as much like April on the high plains as October. So he felt warm enough in just his orange brocaded vest and lavender frock coat as he strode the covered walks that evening.

At the Crystal Palace, things were just commencing to come to life as the working stiffs who dropped by to nurse a beer and talk big went home to their women. Longarm wasn't surprised to see that neither old Duke Roberts nor the sinister crew that rode for him were in town that night. At a corner table, dealing stud, Diamond Donald Dillon didn't seem to miss the D Bar D bunch at all. To look at him now, one would hardly see him as the shark old Duke had bullied out of a four-figure pot the night before. Diamond Donald had changed his planter's hat and treated himself to a Havana Perfecto to get cracking at rebuilding his wealth.

He had four suckers at the table with him, with an empty chair set to mousetrap a fifth. So Longarm drifted over, asked permission to sit in and didn't bother with introducing himself as Jones, now that even the help at his hotel had taken to calling him Mr. Mason. Diamond Donald said he'd heard Frank Mason was in town and softly added he was a straight shooter who hoped it was understood this was a purely friendly game with nobody out to take unfair advantage of his friends.

Longarm could lie just as brass-ass when he had to. So he agreed a man who'd cheat a friend at cards would sell his kid sister to Mr. Lo for a buffalo robe, knowing full well, having watched the night before, he was up against a brass-ass mechanic with more cards up his sleeves than he dealt out in any hand.

That was why Longarm had asked to sit in. It took forever to win enough to matter in an *honest* game.

When Diamond Donald warned him a silver dollar was the minimum ante at that particular table, Longarm hesitated on purpose, shrugged and said he was in, he reckoned, as he tossed his own cartwheel into the five-dollar pot already in situ. He wasn't surprised when Diamond Donald dealt him four treys and a wild deuce, albeit two pair would have been smoother. He leaned back thoughtfully, softly humming "Aura Lee" and raised five. Two of the others saw him, as did Diamond Donald, of course, but the other two folded.

Longarm said, "*Bueno*, I'll raise you another ten, then."

Diamond Donald gently but firmly replied, "No, you won't. I forgot to mention it, but this is a friendly game and you're commencing to raise the roof. So you're covered, I call, and let's see what you're so happy about, Mr. Mason."

Longarm turned his winning hand face up and nobody objected as he raked in the twenty-five dollar pot. But Diamond Donald didn't look at all pleased when his sucker pocketed his winnings and rose from the table, thanking one and all for letting him sit in a hand.

"Just one hand? You mean to quit after winning just one hand?" the chagrined Diamond Donald demanded.

Smiling down pleasantly, Longarm said, "All my dear old daddy left me was an almost empty fifth of Jamaica rum and the advice from one who knew I should always quit when I was ahead."

As he turned away, the tinhorn who'd thought he was priming the pump called out, "Come back here and give your pals the chance to break even, damn it!"

Longarm just kept walking. He wasn't there to improve on the legend of Frank Mason by defending his sportsmanship against a known mechanic. He'd only meant to replenish his pocket jingle without risk in a friendly game.

He moved over to the bar and treated himself to a boilermaker by breaking one of his easily won cartwheels. As he was served a familiar she-male voice purred, "Damned if you're not slick as the shine on that silly Spanish hat! For a minute there, I was afraid Diamond Donald was going to clean your plow for you!"

Longarm turned to smile down at Bulgarian Billie as he replied, "Evening, ma'am. I hope it's understood by the powers that be that I ain't out to take that whole table away from your resident mechanic."

He was too polite to say the light shone slick off her henna-rinsed upsweep, too. She'd likely had a bath before donning that fresh scarlet cancan outfit, too. She smelled like she had.

Bulgarian Billie laughed—she had a pretty laugh—and said, "Those things they say about you must be true. You got balls that would make a brass monkey proud, and I'm sure Diamond Donald must have heard by now how you ran Alamo Jack out of town with his tail betwixt his legs this morning!"

Longarm downed his shot and chased it with a sip of suds before he confided, "That's the trouble with gossip. By the time it gets a couple of furlongs, a jar of olives busted on the walk turns into a wagonload of watermelons hit by a train. I never run nobody out of town, Miss Billie. Me and old Alamo just had us a friendly discussion about his manners. Nobody told nobody to get out of town."

She said, "That's not the way I heard it, albeit there is some dispute as to whether it was you or Duke Roberts who told Alamo Jack to get out of town after you stared down the whole D Bar D!"

He muttered into his suds, but she insisted, "It's all over town, and, speaking as a woman, that was swell of you to stand up for that homely spinster in the railroad depot! They say you didn't know her—before nor after—and you still took her part against a dangerous hairpin backed by half a dozen others! What makes you so sweet to women when you're so hard on men, Frank Mason?"

He chuckled dryly and said, "I've been know to be hard on women."

She laughed a skylark laugh and said, "I may take you up on that if you're still around, and alive, come closing time! But right now I got to sucker some of the other boys for the management. . . . So, maybe later?"

He just smiled and she flounced off in her scandalsome outfit to drink tea water at scandalsome prices with those she had down as poor working stiffs.

It was a caution how some women seemed to cotton to shiftless skunks whilst they looked down their noses at the poor saps who showered them with flowers, books, candies and honorable intentions. Longarm had gotten to the point where he wouldn't have been *too* surprised to hear Miss Lemonade Lucy, the First Lady, had run off on President Hayes with Jesse James. And they said Jesse had a right nice little wife putting up with all his bullshit already!

"I fear I owe you an explanation, sir," said another familiar figure to the other side of Longarm, this one with a deeper voice.

The rider who'd just sat there like a bird on a wire, down at the U.P. Depot, had hair black as stove polish but he hadn't shaved since that morning and his stubble looked like brick dust.

Longarm tried to let him off by allowing he didn't recall anything done to him, adding, "I fear you have the advantage on me, pard. I answer to Frank . . . Mason and, no offense, I don't remember you from nowhere."

The black-haired gent with a red chin stubble said, "Just call me Bob, for now. I can see why you wasn't paying me no mind at the U.P. Depot, earlier today!"

Longarm tried to look surprised as he asked, "Was that you, down to the far end of the counter? You're so right about my feeling too disstracticated to give a damn, no offense. I hope you understand I never knew that lady that rider insulted was with you."

Oregon Bob lied, "She wasn't. The two of us have been staying at the Hotel Custer and she asked my familiar face to escort her home. So I did. That's all I know about her. She seems to be traveling alone, and I suspect she's an old maid from the way you flustered her by standing up to that cuss. I know you won't buy it, but I might have stood up to him my ownself had I been paying more attention. I never knew until I was walking the poor thing back to our hotel that the cuss referred to some part of her anatomy in a manner she was too red-faced to go into in detail."

Longarm just sipped his drink.

Oregon Bob said, "Think what you will. I cheerfully allow I don't like noise as much as you must, Frank. I understand that aside from daring Alamo Jack Aherne to draw this morning, you rawhided a county deputy in front of God and everybody on the streets of Ogallala last night and the less said about earlier shootings in other parts, the better! What makes you so ornery, Frank Mason?"

Longarm shrugged, "I ain't all that ornery. I just don't like bully boys. Never have. Used to be scared of them when I was little. Then I turned out big for my age, practiced some with firearms and you know the rest."

Oregon Bob said, "No, I don't. I just now saw you earn better than two weeks wages for an honest cowhand off a crooked gambler. But you never made toad squat standing up to seven men this morning and I fail to see the profit in sassing a deputy sheriff. I don't suppose you'd care to tell this child what you do for a living when you ain't on the dodge from a shooting charge?"

Longarm said, "You're right. I never asked what *you* do for a living, neither, Bob."

Oregon Bob tried for a jovial expression as he replied. "Let's just say I'm in a line of work that calls for me *avoiding* unpaid arguments with deputy sheriffs or anyone else, as far as possible. There do come times when a man may have to back his requests with a gun muzzle, but you hardly ever have to shoot nobody when you point your gun muzzle in a convincing manner."

Longarm shrugged, signaled the barkeep to pour one for his new found pal, and said, "I dunno, Bob. To tell it true, I've been hoping to meet up with an old . . . business associate who knows how to get a federal warrant torn up. I mean, how was I to know the asshole was a fucking employee of the federal B.I.A. when I only shot him in his fucking leg?"

Oregon Bob brightened and said, "You need a high-powered fixer? By a fortunate turn of fate I'm riding the owlhoot trail with a bird who got life at hard reduced to time served in a federal pen, and if that ain't fixing, I don't know what is!"

Longarm waited until they'd been served and the bar-keep had moved on before he said, "I reckon I'll stick with the pals I know, for now. But just in case the cuss I'm waiting on fails to show . . . What sort of score are we talking about and how might you gents mean to split it?"

Oregon Bob cheerfully replied, "Too early to say. We're discussing a bank the boss is still casing. But every bank in town is awash in cold cash with the fall beef sales in full progress. As to the split, as a rule the boss takes forty percent with the rest of the crew dividing up sixty. If you throw in with us, we'll add up to the four in the bank and a pair of right slick lookouts who don't share in full with us splitting sixty percent. We each slip them a hundred for their time and trouble, regardless of the score, which should add up to at least four figures."

Longarm grimaced and growled, "You expect this child to share one fourth of the risk for little more than an eighth of the take? Thanks, but no thanks. When I share a quarter of the risk I want a quarter of the take, unless your generous boss can assure me he'll hang twice as often as the rest of us."

Oregon Bob helped himself to a heroic swig of his free drink and suggested, "I'll tell the others you demand a bigger cut. I doubt our peerless leader will go for it. But it won't hurt to ask. Why don't you think about it whilst you wait for that pal who knows how to fix a pissy shoot-ing. The pal *I'm* talking about knows fixers who can get a man off murder in the first. Federal!"

He drained his stein and added, "If you change your mind, I'm at the Hotel Custer. Don't ask my room number now or then. Hang around the taproom or the lobby and I'll come to you at midnight, though hell should bar the way."

Longarm didn't comment on how many lookouts they had posted over at the Hotel Custer. He was trying not to look as pleased as he felt, now that he knew where at least some of Lefty Lindwood's gang was holed up.

He said, "I'd feel more comfortable discussing . . . business at my own hotel, the Ogallala Overland Rest."

Oregon Bob said, "We wouldn't. Never you mind why. I'll tell my own pals you're dickering on the split. You may or may not have blown the opportunity already. If you find yourself hanging around our hotel as long as a full hour, it'll mean we're gone and you have. So thanks for the cheer and, like I said, think about our offer."

Longarm did as he found himself drinking alone again. If he headed a raid on the Hotel Custer to find nobody waiting there for him, or even if he ran Oregon Bob in alone, on all he had on him for certain, that invite to do something shifty but uncertain with no proof such an offer had been made . . .

"You're in trouble, handsome," another familiar voice cut through the tobacco haze to confide.

Turning to smile sheepishly at Bulgarian Billie, Longarm said, "So I noticed. Or might we be talking about some other fix I'm in, ma'am?"

She said, "Just now heard Alamo Jack is liquored up and bragging in advance about all the bullet holes he means to put in you. They say he just left the Fighting Sixty-Ninth Saloon for your hotel, with a view to putting all those holes in you from the dark."

Longarm sighed and said, "I just hate a poor loser. Reckon I'll give him some time to come to his senses and then I'll just have to get it on home and see if I can spot him first, thanks to your advance warning."

Bulgarian Billie said, "Least a girl can do for a man who stands up for her kind. But Alamo Jack don't have any senses to come to, and I have a better idea. I get off at midnight, Frank. So why don't you come on home with me and let the asshole lay for you in vain?"

114

Chapter 13

One of the first things Longarm found out about Bulgarian Billie, once they'd wound up bare-assed in bed together after the usual fooling around on her parlor sofa, was that her natural hair color was light brown. Then, as he parted the same with his questing shaft, she warned him she really hailed from Ohio and hadn't liked it at all the one time she'd tried it Bulgarian style with a farm boy hung a lot smaller.

He said he understood as he started gentle in a sham redhead paid to sucker gents with all sorts of bullshit bait. From the way she was moaning and groaning, he was tempted to believe her when she confessed she hadn't been getting any lately. Other gals in her line of work had confided a gal who came regular got rusty at teasing. She allowed giving in to him would have slowed her down at the Crystal Palace a heap had he been a fucking ribbon clerk or cowhand she was fucking that night.

So he knew better than to let her take him for an honest man and a good time was had by all as Bulgarian Billie gave her all to a lowlife no decent gal should have associated with.

Knowing gals with her peculiar taste got most of the

forbidden thrill from the notion they and they alone could *handle* a mean bastard everyone else was scared of, and seeing he was a considerate lover by nature, he thrilled the B girl with a heart of gold by treating her like a lady, or at least like a lady fornicating with a gentleman, and it made her cry when he called her honey and kissed her while he was coming in her.

She shyly confided she'd known all along a man who was so mean to men would naturally know how to treat a natural woman right.

She was full of shit, of course. Longarm had arrested too many no-good bastards who beat on *everybody* to entertain that myth, which, like the one about all bullies being too yellow to hit smaller men who stood up to them, supposed a world the way it *should* have been instead of the way it *was*. But he felt no call to disabuse her of her romantic notions. As she got on top, sliding up and down like a merry-go-round pony with the pole placed sassy, Bulgarian Billie teasingly suggested that he'd come to her place to avoid a shoot-out in the dark with Alamo Jack.

She dimpled down at him in the lamplight. "Fess up, darling man. You passed on the joys of manslaughter in the hopes you'd wind up doing just what you're doing to me this very minute!"

Longarm laughed up at her and pointed out, "At this very minute you are the one having her wicked way with poor, little, helpless me. But to tell the pure truth, I did consider having it out with Alamo tonight and just getting it over with, one way or the other. Now I fear you've made my chore tougher. Because unless he wises up and lights out, there's just no telling when and where he might lay for me next."

She moved her rolicking rump faster and leaned forward to brush her nipples with his moustache as she said she was sorry.

He assured her she was forgiven by inhaling as much

116

of one tit as he could suck betwixt his teeth, then he rolled her on her back some more to finish right. It was easy to finish right, on top, with Bulgarian Billie. For even though she didn't really take it up the ass, she had enough of an ass to where they didn't need a pillow under it to tilt her old ring dang doo at a right welcoming angle.

And so the night went, with him pleasing Bulgarian Bille even more by showing more interest in her life story than that of the Frank Mason he'd barely had time to make up. He knew that when women marveled at mystery men and allowed still waters ran deepest, they were really saying it felt swell when a man let them do most of the talking for a change. It hardly seemed fair, but men and women were in total agreement that the opposite sex talked too damned much.

Having seen that men and women were shortchanged by nature, designed to fornicate longer and more often with desperation than with satisfaction, Longarm had spent more time than most men learning about she-male anatomy. So when he got them into a fork-legged position, where he could run it in and out whilst he strummed her old banjo with a free hand, the professional tease moaned, "Oh, my God, that feels so good. You are so much more understanding than any god who made us poor girls as we are, with that tickle-tassle so far from the loving cup! Where did you learn to do that, Frank? Wait, don't tell me. For it makes me want to snatch her bald headed!"

He soothed, "Nobody I ever did this to before had a sweeter little ring dang doo to return the favor with, Miss Billie."

She told him he was a gallant fibber, which was the simple truth, and asked how long he'd be in Ogallala.

He told her truthfully he didn't know, explaining, "I've been waiting here for somebody uncertain to approach me with a deal I'd as soon not talk about. Have you ever

117

fished for bluegills in a ditch overgrown with duckweed?"

She said, "I told you I grew up on a farm before I went wrong. You're saying you might get a nibble any minute or you might just set there by the ditch indefinite, right?"

He stroked her faster in response to the increasing tempo of her hip thrusts as he said, "Not indefinite, more's the pity. I can't afford to wait that long. But with any luck, we'll have a few more nights like this. Let me kiss you as we top this rise coming up, sweet stuff!"

She moaned, "Ohhh, me, toooo!" as they locked lips to grope for one another's tonsils with their tongues.

As they lay there gasping for air in the afterglow, Bulgarian Billie threatened to beat all previous records for climaxes in one night. But, in the end, they wound up asleep in each other's arms and Longarm had to agree their morning session might not add up, fair, as numbers nine and ten.

Seeing she didn't have to get back to the Crystal Palace before midafternoon, Bulgarian Billie served him a swell breakfast in bed as she begged him to stay at least to noon.

Longarm explained he had an earlier appointment and so after they showered together, she let him get dressed. He said he'd see her later at the Crystal Palace and they kissed on that and parted friendly.

The distance from Bulgarian Billie's hired cottage to the Hotel Custer was too short to bother riding and a bit of a bother to walk. So Longarm was glad the October day had dawned a mite crisp without being cold enough for a topcoat outside.

He ambled along the shady side to pause at a tobacco shop across from the Hotel Custer for fresh claros and yesterday's edition of the *Denver Post*. Papers from Frisco or New York took even longer to get there by rail.

It was all he could do to keep from crying, or laughing out loud, as he scanned his hometown paper for the details of his own swell funeral after laying in state for a spell.

Folk he barely remembered, if he knew them at all, had surely said nice things about their old pal. Nobody seemed to have worried all that much about some bond money the now-late Longarm had been holding in escrow, somewheres, at the time of his far away assassination. You had to look sharp to find the pending suit for recovery among the legal notices under the want ads, filed by a John Watts of Texas against the U.S. Government. So Longarm knew he was well on his way to canonization in the pantheon of the West if he didn't come back to life right soon.

As Longarm suspected, crossing the dusty street in the bright fall sunlight, he was being observed from on high before he could enter the Hotel Custer. But he was banking on the way a wild change of clothes unmade the man one might recall from some time back. He'd met up with more than one old army buddy from his misspent youth in that war his generation had been invited to and had a hell of a time connecting a somewhat older gent in civilian clothes to just which old member of what squad they might be. Nobody Longarm had ever known in or out of the military had ever seen him wearing a Spanish hat with a purple sheen, he felt certain.

Phoebe Blake was posted at the top-story window as their lookout when Longarm broke cover down below. She said, "He's coming, Lefty. That's him in the Spanish hat and sort of lavender frock coat!"

Moving to join her as they both peeked throught the jalousies, the cadaverous Lefty Lindwood marveled, "He's wearing a vest made out of orange peels, too! Bob's right about him looking mighty wild, and do we invite him to ride with us, we got to do something about that flash."

Then Lefty frowned thoughtfully and added, "Hold on, I know that bird from somewheres! I seldom associate with such cheap flash, but there is something about the way he's walking. He don't walk like a cheap flash dressed like a colored pimp. He walks like a man who knows his way through this vale of tears."

Phoebe said, "I told you he knows his way around. If you ask a girl who knows what outward appearances can do for one, I suspect he's dressed like that on purpose because he doesn't want folk who may have seen him wearing *sensible* duds to recognize him easy. Folk who say they know him, here in Ogallala, say he's on the dodge. Didn't he ask Bob about fixing a federal warrant?"

Lefty turned to ask, "Bob?"

Veron looked up from the fashion magazine she was reading to tell Lefty, "Bob ducked out to meet him in the taproom as soon as Phoebe said she'd spotted him. You want me to go down and tell Bob to bring him on up?"

Lefty said, "Not hardly. An unescorted woman in even a hotel taproom would attract just the sort of attention we've been trying to avoid. And I ain't ready to let this Mason see my face until I know him a whole lot better!"

So Lefty went back to dealing solitaire on the bed-spread as Verona studied fashion and Phoebe kept an eye out for any items of further interest. Meanwhile, down-stairs, Oregon Bob and Longarm, pretending to be Frank Mason, bellied up to the bar and ordered straight suds, it being so early in the day.

Oregon Bob asked, "What's this I heard around the Crystal Palace about somebody called Alamo and you, Frank?"

Longarm said, "He was the asshole who insulted that little old spinster gal at the U.P. Depot the other morning. You were there. He made some more war talk last night but, as you see, we're both still alive. You say that shy little thing who asked you to take her home stays at this hotel, Bob?"

Oregon Bob said, "I reckon. Ain't been to bed with her recent. Have you reconsidered throwing in with us, Frank?"

Longarm sipped some suds thoughtfully before he asked, "Throwing in for exactly what? Did you talk to your boss about hogging nearly half the pot?"

Oregon Bob nodded and replied, "He's set in his ways when it comes to money. But I told him about your personal problems, and he's offering to sweeten the deal by fixing that federal charge for you, once we ride out of here with enough to make us all feel rich for a spell."

Longarm sighed and said, "It's a pure caution how short a spell a man can feel rich in a world so filled with temptation. I'll allow I was figuring on spending a bundle on my own fixer. So we might be able to work something out if he could get me a price on this other fixer he knows. What do you all usually pay such a wonder?"

Oregon Bob said, "It depends on how bad a fix needs fixing. I doubt an Indian agent is likely to cost you all that much, dead or alive."

Longarm insisted he wanted some solid numbers, stalling for time in the hope Lefty Lindwood would crawl out from under his wet rock to join them. For he knew that while he didn't have enough on any of the gang to make an arrest stick tight, it was likely they'd turn state's evidence on one another during the seventy-two hours they could be held on suspicion alone.

He knew that they knew only one member of their gang, the one and only one who'd left the murder scene at the Ogallala Overland Rest, alive, that time, would be sweating bullets, alone in one cell.

Accusing all concerned of a hanging offense and locking them up alone would likely loosen *someone's* tongue within seventy-two hours, and one loose tongue was all Judge Dickerson was really after. The judge might even offer the actual killer a deal in exchange for that highly placed fixer he was lusting for.

So they dickered high and they dickered low and after a spell Lefty Lindwood, upstairs, had waited long as he had a mind to and eased down the back stairs for a closer look at this fancy dan in the purple hat.

Knowing the layout of the Hotel Custer, and known by the staff of the same, the cadaverous good tipper made his way out the back and around to the rear of the tap-room, to drift in through the kitchen with a curt nod and some meaningless words of explanation to the kid fixing the free lunch trays back yonder.

Longarm was lounging against the bar with his left el-bow on the same, his gun hand free, facing the street entrance where trouble was most often apt to loom. Hence Oregon Bob, facing Longarm and the back of the joint, spotted Lefty standing in the kitchen door and, from where he stood, Lefty could make out Longarm's profile in the mirror of the back bar. Once he had, Lefty wasn't there anymore.

Oregon Bob said, "Hold the thought. I got to pee, real bad!" and tore out the back to catch up with Lefty on the back stairs and ask him why he suddenly looked so pale.

Lefty Lindwood snarled, "You total asshole! I'll tell you why I look so pale! That swell recruit you or—all right—that fucking Phoebe hold in such high esteem is none other than Deputy U.S. Marshal Custis Long, better knows as Longarm, the very man who pistol whupped me flat and run me in for robbery and murder one that time. And let me assure you, Oregon Bob, one time was enough. Didn't I order you and the boys to *kill* the son of a bitch for me?"

Chapter 14

Oregon Bob laughed incredulously and said, "You did. We did. You got Longarm on the brain, Lefty! I told you right off I wasn't sure we wanted Fank Mason for that bank job. But if there is one thing I am sure of, he surely can't be a haunt! The man me and the boys killed over to that other hotel owned up to being the famous Longarm. They found Longarm's badge and ID on the body ere they shipped it back to Denver, where it was identified as Longarm and buried as Longarm after lying in state like Longarm. Don't you never read the papers?"

Lefty said, "I do, and so who's that son of a bitch in there who looks exactly like the son of a bitch who beat the shit out of me and testified against me at my protracted trial if he ain't Longarm?"

Oregon Bob soothed, "Another tall drink of water with the same brand of mustache and six-gun a body could *take* for an old enemy after years of brooding about the same. Lots of folk look like lots of folk, Lefty. Mayhaps you've hated Longarm so hard for so long that having us kill him once for you wasn't enough to satisfy your soul. But take it from the man who held his gun hand whilst Giggles and Weedy pumped him full of lead, your old pal, Longarm, is dead as a turd in the milk bucket. So about that jasper who just looks like him, waiting out front for me to finish pissing . . ."

Left said, "I don't want him. Get rid of him."

"You mean slap leather on him?" asked Oregon Bob in a thoughtful tone, adding, "I dunno, Lefty. He carries double action and acts like a man who knows how to handle himself seven to one!"

Lefty sighed and said, "I only said get rid of him. Things have just cooled down after that earlier killing and I reckon you must be right about my getting edgy in my old age. I just don't feel right about robbing a bank with a cuss I don't know who reminds me so much of that lawman, dead or alive. Tell him we've called the robbery off. Tell him I took sick or, shit, tell him I'm in a family way, as long as you get rid of him."

Oregon Bob said, "Sounds easy enough. I was having a time talking him into it, anyhow. So who *should* I recruit for the job, if old Frank Mason makes you nervous?"

Lefty said, "Nobody. I just got a wire from Thumbless Mike McNutt, a good old boy I recall from Jefferson Barracks. He'll be joining us by the end of the week with Dinky Cole, a road agent of some experience. The four of us, with the gals on lookout, ought to be enough. So fuck Phoebe's wild man who brings back bitter memories to this child!"

Oregon Bob shrugged, returned to rejoin Longarm at the bar and tell him, "I just had more than a piss in the back, Frank. The boss just now called a change in plans."

Longarm replied, "Do tell? I was afraid you were jacking off all that time. What's the new deal?"

Oregon Bob said, "No deal. Job's off, and we're sorry we wasted your time, Frank."

Longarm tried, "What about that federal fixer you said your boss might fix me up with, Bob? I'm in a real jam, here!"

Oregon Bob said, "Your misfortune and none of my

own, old son. I feel for you, but we're all leaving town and none of us put bullet one in that card playing Indian agent charged to your account. So you're on your own, and if I was you, I'd get a good lawyer or, better yet, get my ass across either border, north or south!"

Longarm didn't try to stop Oregon Bob as he strode away. Longarm had no way of knowing Lefty Lindwood was on the premises of the Hotel Custer and they didn't have enough on Oregon Bob, yet, to sweat him good if he knew he was all alone and fixing to get out in seventy-two hours.

Longarm finished his drink, alone at the bar, while he worked on his next best move. It hardly seemed likely they knew who he really was. Lefty Lindwood had sworn on his mother's head to kill his arresting officer if ever he had the chance and he'd already had that imitation Longarm murdered. So mayhaps Oregon had told the simple truth. . . .

It could happen. It took diligence to lie each and every time.

Longarm decided to sit tight a night or so with Bulgarian Billie and wire Billy Vail for further instructions if nobody changed their fool minds. Longarm knew Lefty Lindwood was a sneaky son of a bitch, with a caution honed by being caught in spite of more-clever-than-average planning. So there was a chance this dismissal was a test, to see what Frank Mason would do on his own.

"An undercover lawman would be heading for the Western Union about now," Longarm decided, snapping a dime on the bar as he turned from it.

He'd meant to leave by way of the lobby, for a better handle on the layout of the Hotel Custer. But before he could, a ten-or twelve-year-old newsboy with a bag of papers slung from one skinny shoulder came in the front way to ask in a piping voice if anyone there might be Frank Mason.

Longarm allowed he sometimes answered to that handle. So the kid told him, "This gent across the way just bet me two bits I couldn't find you in here and tell you he's waiting for you to come on out to join the dance. That's how he put it. I don't know what that means."

Longarm reached in his own pants as he replied, "I reckon I do. Are we talking about a lean, mean-looking jasper in a black riding outfit with his gun riding low in a tied-down holster?"

As he accepted the quarter, the kid said, "Thanks, mister. That's how I might describe him, and he says they call him Alamo Jack. Is he a pal of yours, mister?"

Longarm smiled thinly and said, "Not exactly. I want you to go on into the next-door lobby and see if anyone there wants to buy a paper, kid. This might not be a good time for you to be out on the street."

As the kid went one way, Longarm unbuttoned his frock coat, took a deep breath, and stepped out the front way. The first thing he noticed was that others seemed to have taken his advice about the street out front. Despite it being the middle of a clear sunny weekday, not one critter was stirring the sunbaked dust of the fairly wide thoroughfare.

As Longarm's new Spanish hat cleared the shade of the overhang on his side, a familiar figure broke cover across the way and Longarm could see from the way he was walking, trying to loom ominous, that Alamo Jack Aherne had been lubricating his nerves with something stronger than tea with cream and sugar.

As Longarm strode forth to meet him. Alamo Jack sneered, "I was so afraid you wouldn't be able to make it. Can you guess why I invited you out here, you son of a bitch?"

Longarm stopped near the middle of the otherwise empty street and called back, "Let's leave our mommas out of this and consider how dumb this is, Alamo. I got no good reason to kill you, and I wasn't the one who fired you. So you'd do better looking for another job than waving that fool Schofield around!"

Alamo Jack broke stride four yards away to spread his heels firmly as he snarled, "I aint waving any six-gun, yet. When I reach for it, you can commend your soul to Jesus because your ass will belong to me! I am waiting for you to slap leather before I beat you to the draw, easy. I agree I got the edge on you. But did I ever tell you to buy that slowpoke cross-draw rig?"

Longarm said, "Most of us more serious gun hands favor cross-draw as the best rig for the most positions. I'll allow that tied-down side-draw gives you the edge in a face-to-face-afoot, such as this one. But allow me to offer some friendly advice and don't try it. Like I said, I got no sensible call to kill you, I don't want to kill you, so don't make me kill you, hear?"

Alamo Jack snarled, "You're not going to crawl out of it that easy. You got me fired and, worse yet, more than one fucking gossip has said you backed me down in the U.P. Depot! So here we stand today with the whole world watching, and if you won't make the first move, I will tell you what I'm going to do. I am going to count to ten and then I aim to draw and drill you no matter what!"

Alamo Jack was wrong about the *whole world* watching, but enough people were up on the top floor of the Hotel Custer. Phoebe Blake had called Lefty Lindwood and the others to the window to watch. So there they were as Alamo Jack got to, "Eight, nine . . ." He never made it to ten as the space between them filled with the dazzling white smoke of black powder and the double report of Longarm's derringer.

With his hand on the grips of his still-holstered Schofield, Alamo Jack swayed like a palm in a hurricane, despite the sudden stillness all around, to gasp in a suddenly more sober tone, "How in hell did you ever draw that fast?"

Longarm shifted the empty double derringer to his left

hand as he got out his six-gun, saying, "Nobody draws that fast, cross-draw. That's how come I was holding this derringer, palmed, as I begged and pleaded with you not to make me kill you, Alamo."

Alamo Jack sighed and said, "I reckon I should have listened, for I reckon you just did, and I still say you're a son of a bitch!"

Then, game to the end and hoping he'd be remembered that way, the brave but foolish Alamo Jack Aherne went down like a felled spruce tree to land face up as the dust his fall had stirred up drifted off down the street in the sunlight.

Upstairs, to Longarm's rear, Phoebe Blake was crowing, "You still think my Sir Galahad is the law? Look what he just now did to that fresh cowboy who insulted my ass the other day!"

Oregon Bob said, "Whoever he may be, he surely moves fast. Beat a side-draw with a cross-draw! Did you see how he managed that, Lefty?"

Lefty said, "Not with his back turned to us. Might have used a belly gun."

Verona said, "He's got nice shoulders and a trim butt, too. I vote we invite him back to the party!"

Lefty said, "I don't. We'll know any minute whether he's the real McCoy or not."

So they were watching, unseen from below, as Longarm stood over the body until, sure enough, he was joined in the middle of the deserted street by two county deputies, one of whom he already knew.

The younger, rat-faced Jeb Folsom smiled wolfishly down at the body spread like a welcome mat between them as he chortled, "Well, well, well, what have we here? Didn't you hear me tell you to get out of my county and didn't you tell me to go fuck myself, Frank Mason?"

Longarm mildly suggested, "I never told you to fuck yourself. I only said you didn't have nothing on me that would stick."

Folsom looked as if he was fixing to come in his pants as he said, "That was then and this is now. Turn around and put your hands behind you, killer!"

Longarm replied, "Aw, shit, it was self-defense, front of both sides of this street! Ask anybody in either direction if that drunk on the ground didn't call me out here and declare his intention of drawing on me at the count of ten!"

Deputy Folsom said, "Ain't asking anybody else shit before you turn around and let me cuff you like I just asked. Am I supposed to count to ten before we shoot you for resisting arrest, Frank Mason?"

Longarm muttered, "Aw, bird turds!" as he turned the other way and let the fool kid cuff him, then disarm and pat him down.

Sniffing the still warm derringers, Folsom told his fellow deputy they'd found the murder weapon. He sounded like he believed that, too. Longarm said, "I warned him I had the means to kill him if he didn't cut it out. He insisted on getting shot until I just had to shoot him. Ask any of them folk staring out at us, now!"

Folsom said, "Save your excuses for the judge, killer. County Jail is thataway, to our north. You want to walk it or would you rather get there in the meat wagon?"

Longarm allowed he'd as soon get there under his own power. So he did, with windows popping open on all sides and kids running out in the street for a better look at the infamous Frank Mason as they frog-marched him to the Keith County Jail behind the sheriff's office and handy to the county courthouse.

As they herded Longarm inside, the desk boss asked who he was and what he was charged with. As Deputy Folsom spread the valuables he'd taken off his prisoner across the desk beside his guns, he laughed as mean as a kid writing dirty words on a shithouse wall, "His name would be Frank Mason. They day he shot a man in Denver, I warned him not to try such shit here in Keith County and he just now shot a rider off the D Bar D."

The desk boss whistled and asked, "Shot him serious, Jeb?"

Folsom said, "Twice in the heart, dirty, with a concealed weapon!"

Longarm protested, "Like hell I did! I hit him low enough for him to call me a son of a bitch before he went down. Got him through the aorta, most likely. As to concealed weapons, he knew full well I was armed. He kept challenging me to draw, dad blast it and, by the way, he wasn't riding for the D Bar D no more. That was what the fuss was all about."

The desk boss repeated Deputy Folsom's suggestion he save it for the judge and told a turnkey reading *Captain Billy's Whizz Bang* in a corner to lock the prisoner up out back. So the turnkey tossed his magazine aside and took charge of the handcuffed Longarm, ordering him, not unkindly, to move it on back.

As the two of them did so, the turnkey said, "We feed white bread and beans with water, three times a day. If you want to order real food or coffee from the greasy spoon across the way, I'd be proud to take the price out of your properties envelope for you, as called for."

Longarm said he savvied the unwritten rules of a county jail and had over twenty dollars to last him 'til he got out.

The friendly turnkey said, "I reckon we'll get along. You have anybody here in town you'd like us to get in touch with, for you?"

It was a good question. Longarm wasn't sure he was ready to answer. He knew he could free himself, with sincere apologies, just by letting them know who they had locked up on such a silly charge.

But why would any undercover lawman with a lick of sense want to do a thing like that, just yet?

Chapter 15

Getting locked up on a hanging charge had a lot going for it when you knew you weren't really fixing to hang. You got a private patent cell where you didn't have to listen to crying drunks or fight off bigger gents who said they loved you. It got better once the friendly turnkey supplied Longarm with a thermos of coffee, sandwiches, smokes and some reading material.

The turnkey had marveled at the prisoner's request for that month's issue of *Scientific American* and asked how Longarm, as Frank Mason, had ever learned to read such big words.

Longarm explained, "I never finished school. They gave a war in my honor before I graduated. I can only follow about two thirds of the articles in some of the books I take a crack at. But I figure it's like lifting weights to build up your other muscles. You don't build nothing up unless you try to lift more than you're used to. I see by this month's cover that they just dug up some Egyptian cuss who lived before Jesus Christ and ain't that a bitch?"

The turnkey left him to improve his brain as he saw fit, and it sure beat all how easy it was to follow that article on irrigating the dry southwest by Professor John Wesley

Powell, the one-armed war hero who went down the Colorado through the Grand Canyon ahead of everybody else.

Professor Powell allowed it was possible, but dumb, to irrigate deserts with expensive water, at the taxpayer's expense, to grow thirsty crops like cotton and, for Gawd's sake, rice, when it rained like hell back in the Old South, where fields lay fallow and folk were crying for jobs.

The article about that old time Egyptian had some fancy words that were tougher to figure out. But it was interesting to learn folk had drunk beer and slopped hogs that far back, in spite of the fancy ways they'd posed for those wall murals.

Longarm had just set that magazine aside and picked up the *Police Gazette* to get back to normal when the turnkey said he had a visitor and ushered in a short, plump and perky gal with chestnut curls she had a time keeping up there under that hat as looked like a bird's nest with the damnedest bird he'd ever seen peeking out of it.

She shook through the bars with him as she explained she was a Miss Coletti, a stringer who filed freelance news items for the *Omaha Herald, Kansas City Star* and such.

She said, "No newspaper will hire a girl reporter, full-time, but I guess I've sold a scoop or so in my time. So why do you suppose they mean to hang you when everyone I've talked to said that other man was the one who started the fight, Mr. Mason?"

Longarm shrugged and said, "I don't want my feud with a certain kid deputy to grow into all-out war, Miss Coletti. So let's just say I am saving a full account for the judge, no offense. Coletti ain't a first name if I ask you to call me Frank, is it?"

She dimpled and said, "My friends know me better as Tess, for the stuffier Theresa, Frank. Did I just hear you imply your arrest was a result of that set-to you had with Jeb Folsom near the Crystal Palace the other night?"

Longarm chuckled through the bars at her to say, "You

132

do know your oats as a newspaper reporter, Tess. But please don't file nothing like that before the judge makes them turn me loose. I'd be proud to give you a full interview once I'm *out* of here. But do I need to tell such a . . . woman of the world how hard it can be to get out of jail when the whole courthouse gang is peeved with you?"

She said she followed his drift and added, "I mean to hold you to an exclusive about that man-to-man walkdown, then. For to tell the truth, in spite of all the tales I've read about such gunfights, I have never covered one before. I fear I've been covering the wrong parts of the West."

Longarm shook his head and confided, "No you ain't. What you just now described as a walkdown hardly ever happens. James Butler Hickok had but one, for all Ned Buntline wrote about him, later. They say the late Clay Allison offered to meet Bat Masterson that way on the streets of Dodge. I wasn't there. So all I can say is that for one reason or the other, it never happened. Out our way, in real life, men out to kill one another tend to be more sneaky. Sneaky and smart. For even if one felt he owed a man he hated enough to kill an engraved invitation to a fight, it would be dumb to tell him where he'd be able to fix you in scoped sights from a safe distance at an appointed time and place, see?"

She shook her chestnut curls, insisting, "Why did Alamo Jack send word he wanted to have it out with you in the middle of the street in front of the Hotel Custer if you're so smart about such matters?"

Longarm patiently explained, "Because he was so dumb about them same matters, of course. As we speak he's dead, and I'm not, because I had as much advance warning as it took me to figure the odds and shave them some. I was *tempted* to just duck out the back way, circle further up or down the street, and get the drop on him from behind. I'm sorry, now, I didn't."

She asked, "Why didn't you, then?"

He confessed, "I fear I was showing off. Knowing we were sure to have it out sooner or later, and knowing how so many others in town were waiting to see how it ended, I figured it might be best to just get it over with if I couldn't back him down some more. He'd backed down once and I told him, polite, I was going to kill him if he didn't leave me alone."

Tess Coletti moved her head to get a better look at the prisoner through the bars as she agreed, "That's about the way a newsboy I spoke to earlier saw it. A barber across the street heard you warn Aherne not to go for his gun before you shot him, just as he was . . . For Pete's sake, you're no such person as Frank Mason! Reporter Sparky from the *Herald* pointed you out to me in the courtroom when we were covering that trial in Omaha, Deputy Long! So all this banana oil aside, what are you doing in this Keith County Jail, *Longarm*?"

He started to feed her more banana oil, then he smiled sheepishly and said, "You got me, pard! So can we make a deal, about an exclusive you'll surely sell to the *Chicago Tribune*? I fear I've already made a deal like so with Reporter Crawford of the *Denver Post*."

She moved closer to the bars—it sure smelled nice— to whisper, "I just *knew* there was more to that shoot-out than, well a shoot-out. Are you working undercover on something bigger?"

Before he could answer, her green eyes saucered and she gasped, "Oh, of course! You're here to find out who murdered you last week! I mean to say I see they murdered somebody else and now doesn't *that* explain those charges against a well-known lawman, filed by what I had taken for Texas malcontents out to shake the damn Yankee Justice Department down with false claims about bond money!"

Longarm warned, "Easy, there, girl! You've taken the bit in your teeth and before you gallop to perdition, let's eat this apple one bite at a time! Do we have us a deal that you'll hold off on who I really am until I'm out of here and then some?"

She asked, "How much then some?" She was sharper than she looked under such a hat.

He said, "Ain't certain. Got to get out, got to see if my being in jail a spell has changed any minds about accepting me as the owlhoot rider I'm pretending to be. All I can promise for certain is that I'll tell you the whole story, first, if you don't spoil my surprise ending."

He let that sink in before he added, "It's a free country. I can't keep you from letting my cat out of the bag. But once you do, the mice will vanish into the woodwork and neither one of us will have much of a tale to tell, see?"

She said she did and asked if there was anything she could get for him or anyone she could contact for him. He told her he was set. He didn't know her well enough to entrust her with secret messages for his home office. He *hoped* she was smart enough to see how filing any half-ass report early would be awfully dumb. But dumb people were the ones who caused most of the trouble in his best of all possible worlds.

She promised to keep his secret and left, walking sprightly with her heels clicking sassy on the cement.

After that, it got quiet as hell for a spell and as it started to get dark out, Longarm learned he was expected to pay for lamp oil as well as other added comforts in his cozy boiler plate cell.

Then the same turnkey brought another she-male visitor back to see him. Longarm had to peer intently through the bars in the now-tricky light to see it seemed to be that timid little sparrow from that U.P. lunch counter, for Gawd's sake.

She said her name was Phoebe Blake and that she felt just awful about him having to fight that same villain over her again.

Longarm was too polite to say he hadn't been thinking about her as Alamo Jack had been counting slow but steady to ten, that afternoon.

She didn't strike Longarm as a lady who was used to gents dueling for her favors. When you stared hard through the veil she had hanging off her rusty black hat, her features were regular enough. He figured she'd have been almost pretty had she known how to gussy up a mite.

Since she didn't, Longarm gallantly replied, "I was only doing what I had to, Miss Phoebe. We both heard what he said to you the other day, so there's no need to repeat it. I wasn't trying to show off. I was brung up to respect ladies and, seeing you had nobody else there to stand up for you . . ."

She looked as if she was fixing to cry as she sniffed and said, "A lot you know! The escort I was there with sat like a bump on a log as you and you alone stood up for me! But that ain't what I'm here for."

He asked what she was there for.

She said, "Me and the one you know only as Bob both work for a boss I've no need to mention by name. He wanted me to come over here and . . . see how you were."

Longarm said, "I reckon I'll do all right, as long as my money holds out. Had a lucky run at cards last night. But I reckon I sure could use that fixer Bob knows, right now."

Phoebe said, "That's another reason I'm here. Our boss told me to tell you he's sorry if he misjudged you and to explain that the fixer to which Bob referred has no pull with the local courthouse gang. He ain't based in Nebraska at all. He can only fix state courts in Kansas or federal courts, *some* federal courts, all across the country."

Longarm sighed fatalistic and said, "Reckon my only hope is the old pal I told your Bob about, then. How was I to know they'd be such poor losers about a local boy who told everybody in town he was fixing to clean my plow?"

Phoebe said, "I feel terrible about that, knowing the fight was over my ass. I'd be proud to offer you some of the same if it wasn't for all these bars between us, Frank. Is it all right to call you Frank?"

He chuckled fondly and said, "I don't care what anybody calls me as long as it ain't late for breakfast and I'm sure flattered by your kind offer, Miss Phoebe. But, no offense, I never told that bully to take his unkind remark about your ass back because I was out to seduce you."

She stood straighter, that looked better, and preened, "I was *hoping* that was how you felt about me! For to tell the truth, I've met mighty few men who were willing to stand up for me, pure, like one of them tin men who used to ride for King Arthur! Are you trying to tell me, right out, that if I was to get down on my knees right now and offer to suck you off through these bars you'd say no?"

"I'm afraid I'd have to!" Longarm laughed.

Before he could add that the turnkey came back every twenty minutes or so, the drably dressed but trim-figured Phoebe crowed, "Oh, Jeez, *thank* you, Frank! It makes me feel so swell to be respected like a fucking lady!"

Then she covered her face with her hands, said she had to go, and lit out bawling like a baby for whatever reason.

Longarm figured it was just as well. It was a pain in the ass when you had to arrest a gal and her lawyer brought up her sucking you off in open court.

He tried not to think about her offer as she scanned the pink pages of the *Police Gazette* with its realistic halftones of gals in pink tights. It was early, yet, but he'd had a tough day and so, seeing he was paying for that lamp oil, he trimmed the lamp and flopped on the bunk in the darkness in just his shirt, pants and socks to stare up at nothing much as he tried to fit the pieces together.

The mousy little Phoebe Blake leaving the U.P. Depot with Oregon Bob made more sense, now. So what had they been doing there that morning? Sure, they'd been following him and Salome Morrigan. It made Longarm feel swell to know they'd been respecting Frank Mason before Oregon Bob had contacted him. So how come they'd shied away like that? Right, they'd decided he really was a crook when the other lawmen threw him in jail. So how was he supposed to get out of jail without telling anybody he was the law, his ownself?

He was still studying on that when lantern light lanced through the bars to paint zebra stripes on the back wall as the turnkey called out in a jovial tone, "Drop your cock and grab your socks Mr. Mason. I hate to be the one to tell you this, but you don't get to spend the night in jail after all!"

As he rose from the cot, he was told to gather up all the shit he could take with him. As he pulled on his boots and donned his frock coat, he asked who'd made his bail.

The turnkey said, "Nobody bailed you out. The charges have all been dropped. Can I have that *Police Gazette* if you're done with it?"

Longarm left all the reading material, the lamp oil and a quarter of the coffee in the thermos to the next unfortunate and followed his pal out front, where the night desk was jawing with a familiar figure in black, wearing his own Schofied, low and tied down.

As Longarm joined them with a wary smile, the rider who'd been down at the U.P. Depot with the late Alamo Jack and Duke Roberts nodded to him and said, "I'd be Lash Larson. I owe my new postiton to you. The boss just had a word with his pal, the sheriff, and wants us to carry you out to the D Bar D now. Let's go. Your spare pony's out front with the rest of the boys."

Longarm asked the night desk about his own guns. Lash Larson told him, "We carried it out front for you, Mr. Mason. You'll get it back when the boss tells me to give it back. Let's go."

Longarm couldn't come up with anything more polite than, "No, thanks. I got other plans in town, tonight."

Lash Larson said, "No, you don't. Boss said to bring you out to the D Bar D. So that's where me and the boys mean to take you, friend."

Chapter 16

The night desk returned what was left of Longarm's pocket jingle and everything he'd had in his pockets, save for his double derringer. He didn't ask Lash Larson who had that in safekeeping for him. As they went out front, the night was crisp and the starry sky was cloudless. The damned full moon was rising like a fat old Chinese lantern to the east. Longarm figured his best bet, once he was mounted up, would be a break for it smack in the middle of town, zigzagging around corners. For the last place he wanted to ride on a moonlit night had to be out across the open range with four other pals, he saw, of the late Alamo Jack!

Lash hadn't said and Longarm hadn't asked why the cattle baron Alamo Jack had been working for had put the fix in with a county he swung so much weight in. Cattle barons could be real pains in the ass, once they got used to being the biggest frogs in their puddles.

One of the others was holding a palomino barb for him, damn it. Pale horses made swell targets in bright moonlight. But a man worked with what they gave him to work with, so he was about to mount up when a familiar bird called out to him. So he paused with one foot up in the stirrup to reply to the pleasingly plump gal under the crazy hat, "How do, Miss Tess, and where might we be going, now, so late in the evening, if you don't mind my asking?"

Tess Coletti said, "I was just about to ask you the same question. I just heard they'd dropped those murder charges against you, Mr. Mason. I was on my way here for another interview, but, seeing you're busy . . ."

Not looking at Lash nor the others, Longarm told her, "I got to ride out to the D Bar D, I'm sure you've heard of, to thank your own Duke Roberts for putting in a good word for me. I reckon he must have told the sheriff he fired Alamo in the first place for starting up with me over nothing. But I'd be proud to tell you all about it if you'd care to interview me over lunch, like we'd already agreed, come tomorrow?"

As he'd hoped, she was quick-witted, as well as curious. She nodded, making that dumb bird flap its dumb wings, and said, "The restaurant at the Ogallala Overland Rest, as we'd agreed, at say one o'clock?"

He said he'd be there, Lord willing and the creeks didn't rise, and added as an afterthought, "Would you mind a question that's been on my mind since first we met, Miss Tess?"

She dimpled up at him and said she hoped it was personal. He laughed and said, "It is. I've rid high and I've rid low, from Canada down to Mexico and far east as New York City. But I'll be whipped with snakes if I have ever seen a bird like that one nesting in your hat, ma'am!"

She smiled proudly and said, "Thank you. It's a bird of paradise and I'd feel awfully foolish if birds as expensive could be seen in these United States or even Old Mexico!"

Some of the others were grinning, now, as Longarm ticked his Spanish hat brim to her and forked himself aboard the palomino with a last word about that lunch back there in town.

Trusting Lash Larson to have a lick of common sense had a mad dash on a strange bronc beat. But by the time they'd ridden north past the outskirts of town, Longarm sincerely hoped he'd made the right choice. For that big fat moon had the summer-kilt short-grass lit up silvery as far about as a saddle gun could range, and all five of the black-clad rascals were riding with saddle guns.

The Nebraska plain spread flat to gently rolling without a lick of cover as far as the eye could see. Somewhere in the night a haunting locomotive was moaning, "Come away with meeeeeee!" Longarm sure as hell admired that notion as they rode on, strong and silent or brooding murdersome thoughts for what seemed a million miles.

But it couldn't have been more than five, for, riding at a trot, it took less than an hour to top a last rise and behold the home of the D Bar D, which stretched out along the far side of a draw, with the moonlight painting its elephant-iron roofing silver and lamp light piercing its thick, sod walls all around.

As they rode in, a front door opened and four more figures, short to tall, came out on the veranda to meet them as they rode on in.

On the terse command of Lash, the four other riders peeled off to get on over to the stables with all six ponies, once he and Longarm had dismounted.

As he followed Lash across the yard to the veranda, he saw the familiar bulk of Duke Roberts loomed above the trimmer figure of a gal and two boys of, say, six and eight, both wearing wooly chaps and junior-sized ten-gallon hats, which in point of fact wouldn't hold a gallon if full-sized.

As he and Lash joined them, Duke Roberts held out a hamlike paw to say, "It was good of you to accept my invite, Frank." Then he turned to the gal and said, "Miss

Una, this would be Frank Mason, the gent I told you about when you and the boys arrived too late for the fun the other morning."

Una Clarke née MacAlpin had been West long enough to hold out a hand to be shook not kissed, and she told Longarm she admired a gentleman who insisted on respect for her kind.

Then Duke said, "I'll walk Lash on over to the bunkhouse whilst Miss Una acts as the lady of the house, Frank. You all go on in for some joe and vittels. I'll only be a minute."

The woman flustered, "Duke, I'd hardly call myself the lady of this house! We've barely arrived!"

The jovial owner of all he surveyed replied, "Do you see any other lady of this house, Miss Una? Like I said, I'll be right back."

So she, Longarm and the two boys went on in as their hulking host strode off with Lash to compare notes on how things might have gone in town. Longarm had figured they would.

Under lamplight in the baronial setting room of the main house, Una Clarke née MacAlpin turned out to be a still mighty handsome woman in her late thirties or early forties, with well kept raven's wing hair as shone like wet black paint under lamplight and the bare beginnings of a double chin. Longarm had already noticed she still had her figure, and now he saw her full skirts and tailored bodice were a mostly leaf-green Scotch plaid. So she was no longer in mourning for anybody.

The two kids looked much the same, save for their shirts being army blue and their kerchiefs being yaller. Miss Una introduced her elder son as Angus and allowed the younger one answered to Ian. You got the impression she was second-generation American at best, albeit she was able to talk American without sounding like she had a head cold. Her tone was embarrassed as she waved

Longarm to a sofa near the cow-chip fire in a fireplace either of her boys could have stood up in. She confided, "The boys and me are only guests here, like yourself, Mr. Mason. My late husband and Duke rode together in the war. In the Union Cavalry, in case that matters to you."

Longarm set his Spanish hat aside as he soberly assured her, "It's a mite late for anybody to be brooding about who did what, way back when, ma'am. I disremember which side I rode for when all of us were young and foolish."

The youngest boy came over to stare uncertainly down at Longarm and demand, "Are you a cowboy, mister? How come you got on an orange vest and a purple coat if you're a cowboy?"

His mother blushed and stammered, "Ian! Mind your manners! Do you hear this gentleman asking why you're dressed up as if to round up cows when it's past your bedtime?"

"I don't want to go to bed, Mom. I want to round up cows with that swell pony Uncle Duke says I can ride as soon as he teaches me how!"

The grinning brat turned to Longarm to confide, "I have named him Bonnie Prince Charlie and he's brown and white and he's mine, all mine, so there!"

Angus piped up, "Uncle Duke gave me a pony, too, and I already know how to ride!"

Longarm was saved from having to congratulate them both when big Duke Roberts came back in, holding out Longarm's gun rig as he said, "Lash says he's sorry he forgot to give this back to you, Frank."

As Longarm rose to accept his derringer as well as his .44-40, Duke told Miss Una, "They handed Frank's weapons over to my boys when they let him out this evening. I told all at suppertime about the fool way they treated an innocent man."

The boys exchanged knowing looks. This time it was

Angus piping up to ask, "Are you the gunslick who shot Alamo Jack? What does it feel like to shoot a man? I can't hardly wait to grow up and shoot somebody!"

Their mother jumped up to gasp, "That's quite enough out of both of you spoiled things! It's off to bed we go and Momma will tuck you in if you know what's good for you!"

As the three of them left, Longarm put his six-gun back on but remained on his feet, smiling uncertainly.

Duke said, "Let's go out on the veranda some more, Frank. It's warm out and I'd like a word with you in private."

Glad to be wearing his .44-40, even though he hadn't had a chance to see if it was still loaded, lest he seem impolite, Longarm followed the just-as-tall and way-wider man outside and accepted the fine cigar Duke offered with a nod of thanks.

He returned the favor by lighting both their smokes with one of his own waterproof Mex matches, making casual mention of his regrets about the late Alamo Jack.

Duke Roberts said, "Alamo was an asshole, even before I fired him. I'd warned him not to start things and expect the rest of us to back his play. You were at the U.P. Depot when he started things, anyway. So when I heard they'd run a stranger in for killing him fair in an election year, I warned the district attorney that me and everybody who does what I, damn it, *tell* them to do would vote Democrat next month, after I had appeared at your trial to testify Alamo was after you, premeditated. But what the hell, you're out, it's over, and that ain't why I asked you to come out here this evening, Frank."

Longarm said he'd sort of figured as much.

The burly stockman said, "For openers, I can always use a man who knows how to use a gun and knows better than to use it foolish."

Longarm modestly replied, "I've sort of outgrown working cows, Duke, no offense."

His host shrugged and said, "It was worth the try. If the truth be known, I ain't as concerned with your future as my own."

Longarm said he wasn't much of a fortune teller, either.

Duke said, "Mebbe not, but you are sure as hell a hand with the ladies! I understand you'd just seen a swell looking gal off at the U.P. Depot when you got into it with Alamo over that other gal. Then they say you went over big, and mayhaps went other places with a B girl at the Crystal Palace who don't put out for the rest of us mortals in spite of her bedroom eyes and dirty name."

Longarm didn't answer. Duke said, "In case you never noticed, one of the boys who likes red pepper tells me one of the Mexican gals working across from your hotel is in love with you. Lash says that they told him at the county jail you'd had not one but two she-male visitors before they could turn you loose. So what's your secret and don't tell me it's that loud vest, Frank!"

Longarm said, "For what it's worth, I hardly ever call a lady 'sis' and order her to move her ass before I've known her some, in a biblical sense."

Duke snorted, "Shit. I got better manners than Alamo Jack. We *all* got better manners than Alamo Jack. Did you hear me talking disrespectful to Miss Una in there just now?"

Longarm said, "Not hardly, albeit she did make mention of her boys commencing to act spoiled."

The cattle baron shrugged and said, "I'm their godfather and every kid on Earth wants somebody to give them a pony. I got livestock coming out of my ass and neither pony cost me nothing."

Longarm knew better. No cattle outfit kept Shetland stock in their remuda. And Duke'd bought those scaled down cowboy outfits either by mail order or in town to send to them, in care of their nice looking mother. But he held the thought and let Duke go on, "I like the boys, sincere, and I mean what I told Miss Una about being willing to treat 'em as my own for as long as the three of them might care to stay. What I'd like you to tell me is how a man such as I might go about getting them to *stay*, for *keeps*."

Duke Roberts shifted his weight awkwardly and explained, "I've never been one for courting. I was too busy building up this spread when I got out of the army as an old cowhand with barely two nickels to rub together. I ain't no sissy. I reckon I've fucked my share of fancy gals, but I never married up. I never wanted to marry up with . . . nobody out this way, as soon as I laid eyes on the bride of my old army buddy, Angus Clarke!"

Longarm asked, "Was her man Scotch, too? I'd figured her oldest boy was named after maternal kin."

Duke said, "All three of us were born with Scotch names. But that ain't why I envied my old pal so, going on a dozen years before I heard he'd died of a heart stroke, even though he was so much younger and, well, prettier than me."

He suddenly blurted, "I'll have you know I never tried to flirt with my old army buddy's woman after he asked me to be the godfather for both his boys! I've *yet* to flirt one time with Miss Una, and that's the trouble, Frank. My intentions are pure as the driven snow. I want to marry up with her and leave all I own to her and her boys if only I could have me a wife like that for just a spell. But I fear she thinks of me as a sort of fucking *uncle* or even worse, her dear old dad! So I need the advice of a man who knows the way the minds of women work!"

Longarm sighed and said, "Duke, I'm a man, and *women* ain't too sure about the way women's minds work. But for what it's worth, I can offer a few words of advice about the deadlier of our species."

148

Duke sounded like an eager schoolboy when he said he was all ears.

Longarm said, "You might be trying too hard. Women know, better than we do, the main difference betwixt a lady and a whore is common sense. A whore gives her all three ways for three dollars whilst a lady can expect to be supported for the rest of her natural life for giving in to just one gent now and again."

Duke Roberts growled, "Are you calling my intended a whore, you Gawd damned gun-toting pimp?"

Longarm said, "You just heard me imply she was a lady, Duke. A lady don't want anybody to think she can be bought. So if I was you, I'd back off on expensive presents 'til she and her boys settle in to get used to you and the D Bar D."

"Then what?" asked the owner of the same.

Longarm said, "Then, provided you ain't fucked up by scaring her off, you'll just have to take your beating like a man. She never would have come to join you if she hadn't already considered marrying up again."

Chapter 17

The feather bed in a guest room of the D Bar D had that cot in the county jail beat by a mile and they served their sausage and flapjacks with genuine maple syrup mail-ordered from back East. The two Clarke kids wanted to ride into town with Longarm, but their mother told them they had to learn to ride before they rode half that far. So Longarm rode in alone aboard another D Bar D bronc he left to be picked up later at the municipal corral and strode back to the Ogallala Overland Rest in restored spirits, looking forward to that lunch with Tess Coletti.

But the chestnut-headed reporter gal had left a note for him at the hotel desk, allowing she'd read the menu of the restaurant next door and suggesting they get together at her place, over real food.

Longarm had been hoping folk he was more interested in might have left him a note, now that he'd proven to that little sparrow gal, at least, he was a fellow rider of the owlhoot trail.

It wasn't that he wasn't interested at all in Tess Coletti, he being a natural man and her having high heels that clicked so sassy. But he'd been hoping to be spotted in the restaurant next door and so, seeing he wasn't going to be, he read the morning papers in the hotel lobby and then walked slow on the sunny side of the street past the Hotel Custer, out of his way, on his way to the address Tess Coletti had left him.

When he got there, it turned out to be a carriage house, with her quarters up above the space someone else had hired for storage. A heap of carriage houses near the centers of growing towns got converted like so.

When Tess greeted Longarm at the head of her stairs, he saw she'd let her curly chestnut hair down and had on a bathrobe of Turkish toweling in a harmonizing shade of tan. She was standing there in matching mules with pom poms. He saw he must have caught her just out of her bath and said he was sorry for showing up early.

She dimpled up at him to say, "You're right on time. I've got our *pastae fagioli*, simmering on the back of my stove and the Mexican red ink they had on sale goes close enough with my dago cooking. Come on in and tell me all about that dirty old man and the young widow they say he sent away for, like a fancy pair of Justin boots!"

Longarm followed her into her artistic looking quarters, draped with Hindu curtains and prints of still lives done in that new French style as looked sort of careless. As he took off his hat, he told her Duke Roberts and the Widow Clarke had known one another for years and both were Scotch-American, so what the hey.

Tess turned in the kitchen doorway to ask if that had been meant as a crack about other hyphenated Americans. He said he didn't know what she was talking about. She pouted about taking a lot of teasing about her wop name, out here so far west of New York, New Orleans and other dago towns.

He shrugged and said, "There's enough Eye-talians out our way, I reckon. Last white man to see Custer alive was his bugler, Trooper Martin or Martini. And Charlie Siringo, the Texas range detective, is a man one teases at his own peril."

He let that sink in and added. "If you ever get lonesome, there's a whole town of Eye-talian gold miners out California way. They call the town Sheep Ranch, after the mine they work for. . . . And is that your busted fall ghouls as smells so fine, Miss Tess?"

She trilled, "*Pastae fagioli*, you big silly!" and ducked into her small kitchen to putter around and come back out with two heaping plates of what looked like macaroni mixed with Boston beans to Longarm.

She spread the plates on the coffee table in front of him and said she'd be right back with the silver service and that red ink. When he asked if he could help, she told him her kitchen was a mess she meant to keep her own little secret.

It only took moments before she was seated beside him on the love seat and, as they dug into her hearty notion of a lunch, it got easy to see why that hip, brushing his own from time to time as she shifted her weight to gobble or pour, felt so pleasingly plump.

Her down-home mix of macaroni and beans, cooked in a swell sauce, was filling as well as tasty. The dry sherry she'd chosen with more care than she let on washed it down swell. He noticed that despite being smaller than him, she was eating and drinking more than he was, faster. But it was a free country and he figured to be moving on before she managed to get too fat. He'd noticed in other parts how gals who stuffed themselves like so tended to be free and easy about their other appetites. It was hardly fair, but facts were facts and that was the secret reason many an experienced cocksman was willing to walk down the street with a gal as broad across the hips as a cow. They figured it was worth their shame, once they got her to spread those elephant legs.

When he turned down second helpings with a warning

pat at his orange vest, she said she'd been meaning to watch her own figure and carried the dishes and service out to dump in her kitchen sink. Then, she rejoined him on the love seat to pour more red ink and demanded, "Now I want you to tell me why you are here in that clown suit, as Frank Mason when we both know you're the famous Longarm I've heard so much about!"

He confided, "As I told you at the jail last night, Miss Tess, it is true I'm working undercover on a federal case and you have my word I'll not say a word to another reporter here in Ogallala before I tell you what I just wrapped up, once I wrap it up. I haven't even told another lawman, or even my home office, what I'm on to here in these parts. The killing of that stranger in my place was just icing on a bigger cake."

She commenced to tickle him as she giggled, "Tell me, tell me, tell me about that big old cake, you big old tease!"

Longarm begged her to cut that out and, when she wouldn't, he grabbed her to tickle her back. Tess squealed like a pig and reached lower and tickled his balls. He responded in kind with a grab at her crotch inside her now wide-open kimono. But she refused to stop and she threatened to bite him where it would really hurt as she fumbled with his fly buttons, demanding he tell her what he was doing there.

Longarm told her it seemed plain as day what he was doing there and it didn't hurt at all when she hauled his old organ grinder out, gasped in mingled surprise and admiration and commenced to suck it the way only a gal with a healthy appetite knew how.

So he let her have her wicked way with him and, by the time he'd come, he had them both undressed so he could come the second time in her hot wet ring dang doo with her saying she was coming, too.

Then she asked if he'd mind picking her up off the rug

and going to bed with her, where it wouldn't be so hard on her tailbone.

So he did and that felt better on his knees as well. But no matter how she wriggled and tickled, he held out on telling her what he was really up to in Nebraska. And a grand time was had by all until the rumble of heavier traffic out front warned him it was quitting time in Ogallala, with the sun fixing to go down and the action about to pick up along the owlhoot trail.

The warm-natured newspaper gal wanted to tag along if she couldn't get him to stay the night. She tried some pouty tears and, when that didn't work, she laughed and allowed he seemed serious about his own line of work as she was about hers. So they parted friendly with a kiss at the head of her stairs, seeing she was in no shape to follow him on down to the alley in broad daylight.

So as he headed up the alley, walking sort of stiff, Tess went to a window to yell after him like a nagging wife that she expected him to come back with at least two columns for her to file, bless his heart!

Gals who nagged like nagging wives after a man had only fucked 'em once assured Longarm he'd been right to rein in the few times he'd been tempted to surrender to the unfair sex.

By then, thanks to all that exercise to settle their *pastae fagioli*, Longarm was starting to get hungry again and Tess had been right about the menu at his hotel restaurant offering nothing all that tempting. So he decided that, seeing the famous Longarm was dead and Frank Mason had been firmly established as a knock-around cuss who got arrested even when everyone could see he'd been in the right, he'd risk a bowl of *menudo* followed by *chiles rellanos con tortillas* for mopping up.

He suspected at least one of the gals who worked there really *was* in love with him as he enjoyed the first fully satisfying meal he'd had since leaving Denver. He was having his second coffee with their swell candied cactus cake when Oregon Bob came in to say, "I've been looking all over for you since we heard your own fixer got you off on that killing, Frank! Where the hell you been?"

Knowing that could be a trick question, since he'd ridden in on a D Bar D bronc and left it at the municipal corral, Longarm truthfully replied, "Visiting with the folk who got me out of jail. I wasn't the one who fixed Keith County. I still *need* a fixer. I got help from that big stockman who'd witnessed that brush I had with Alamo Jack— you were there, but I reckon you had your reasons. He came forward to tell the district attorney that Alamo Jack had bragged he was out to clean my plow and wasn't no more welcome in these parts as I was, seeing he was dead with no friends whilst I was innocent and *had* some friends who'd be voting come November."

Oregon Bob shrugged and said, "Whatever. Seeing you got off, and seeing others were watching when you sure cleaned that cowboy's plow, the boss told me to tell you it's on for tonight and to ask if you want to be in or out."

Rising from his table to pay for his supper and tip whichever of the two gals loved him with half a cartwheel, Longarm suggested they take it outside if they meant to discuss such serious business.

Leading Oregon Bob along the walk to the front of a dress shop shut for the night, Longarm said, "I'd like to know what sort of a job we'd be pulling before I decide whether I aim to be in or out, Bob. To tell the pure truth, I've seldom heard of a bank being robbed after closing time."

Oregon Bob said, "We're not holding nothing up. One of our new . . . business associates is a famous yegg man I am not at liberty to name at present. So like the boss asked me to ask you, are you in or out?"

Longarm smiled thinly and said. "You remind me of those gals you meet up with at a Sunday-go-to-meeting cake sale. The ones who coyly hold back on what might or might not be there, waiting up for 'em, if they mayhaps let you walk them home after you bid another asshole on a cake that may or may not taste like shit."

Oregon Bob said, "Suit yourself. I didn't know you were a man of independent means. You remind me of a piss-pot sniffer who demands a doctor's certificate, proving she's a she-male, before he bids on her fucking cake!"

"I just like to know what I might be getting into," Longarm replied.

Oregon Bob snorted, "I just said that. What do you take us for, a sheriff's posse out to entrap you into a vault job?"

Longarm asked, "Is that what you're fixing to rob, a bank vault, at night after they've all gone home?"

The redheaded outlaw with his hair dyed black swore and said, "Shit, no. We're bringing in a famous yegg man to hold the horse out front for us. The boss you'll only meet later tonight if you're in is a man who thinks on his feet. That's how come he's our boss. We were fixing to make our withdrawal the rude way when the bank he'd picked cased out with a walk-in vault set in solid cement with a Mosler time lock. But when a replacement for a gun we'd lost turned up with a sidekick who'd be able to crack the tomb of Prince Albert, if he had a mind to, our boss decided it made more sense to make our withdrawal in the middle of the night with nobody the wiser until we are all of us clear with all of their money. Boss says we're going to need a buckboard to carry off all the paper and specie they'll have on hand to cover the beef checks being written right and left this fall!"

Longarm whistled softly and said, "I'm in. But what do you need my gun hand for if it's going to be a pussy-foot in and a creep-away out?"

Oregon Bob explained, "No way to crack a vault as big as that one in dead silence. The yegg we've recruited to do so says he can muffle the blast pretty good if we haul some mattresses in aboard that same buckboard. But even if we don't wake up the town, some night owl staggering down the street from either direction might wonder what that thump was and come nosing in for a look-see. So the boss wants guns posted out a ways as well as around the buckboard and, of course, the forced entrance. We got two gals to steady the buckboard. I'll cover the door as the boss and the yegg man work inside, at first. You and that other gun hand I just mentioned will be spread out to secure the whole block."

Longarm asked what he'd meant by "At first."

Oregon Bob said, "Once the vault's blown open, once we see nobody else wants to horn in, it's going to take all five of us men to load all the loot aboard the buckboard with one gal holding the team steady and the other holding the ribbons from the sprung seat. Is that enough for you, you piss-pot sniffer, or do we have to draw you a fucking diagram on a fucking blackboard?"

Longarm said, "I get the picture. I don't suppose you'd care to tell me where we'll be meeting, or which of the banks in town we'll be hitting, at what time?"

The known killer calmly replied, "I can't. I don't know. As you get to know him, you'll see you're working with a mighty cunning henhouse fox. All you need to know now is that the boss told me to tell you if you're in he wants you to change into some more sensible dark duds and be in the alley behind the Crystal Palace at midnight on the nose. One of us will meet you there to lead you to the next fork in the primrose path. It may be me. It may be somebody else. We all know what *you* look like. The boss would just as soon you weren't too certain about us until you're in too deep to back out and carry tales to the teacher. Are you still in?"

Longarm said "I reckon. Twelve, straight up, behind

the Palace in my rough riding gear, and I can hardly wait to meet such a shy little thing!"

Oregon Bob sidled off in the gathering dusk without offering to shake.

Longarm muttered after him, "Up your own ass and how is a poor, honest lawman supposed to head off a serious felony without scaring the gang off too soon, or take part in compounding a felony he won't be allowed to testify about in court if he *does* get the drop on the whole gang without getting killed? Seeing he don't know what half of 'em *look* like?"

Chapter 18

Longarm had only brought that one hat, and all the shops had shut down for the night. But where in the U.S. Constitution did it say you had to wear a hat on an early October night? He'd thought to pack a blue army workshirt and a pair of clean but faded jeans. Once he put his emergency peacoat over his gunbelt and less fancy outfit up in Room 2-F, he figured he looked too tough to identify, late at night away from lamplight.

He'd taken his own sweet time and he still had hours to kill before it would be midnight. He went down to the taproom and defended himself for looking so funny to the boys around the card game in the corner.

He confided to Doc he was fixing to crack a safe at midnight and ordered plain draft. Doc thought that was pretty funny. Spats Gordon called out that he'd always figured Frank Mason for a cat burglar, seeing he sure wasn't a sporting man.

Longarm was tempted to lose a hand at blackjack to remember him by if he never came back from his midnight meeting in a dark alley. But he decided it made more sense to scout said alley well before midnight.

That killed more time, albeit all he found out back of

the Crystal Palace was gritty cinders, ash cans and and a tabby cat in heat with half the toms in town yowling up at her as she hissed down at them from the top of a backyard shithouse.

Timing it with care, he circled to enter the Crystal Palace before midnight, order another plain draft and wait for Bulgarian Billie to join him at the bar.

"Were you with another woman last night?" she demanded right out, adding, "I know you got arrested. But they told me you got out of jail by moonrise and I was waiting and waiting. Who is she, damn your fickle heart!"

Longarm soberly assured her, "You have my word I never spent last night with no other gal." And that was the simple truth when you studied on it. So he continued, "I was afraid you'd think something like that. So I came by before you got off to explain why I can't carry you home tonight, neither."

Her voice dropped ten degrees as she answered, "Oh? You've suddenly discovered the joys of self abuse? What's this all about, Frank?"

He said, "You don't really want to know, in case the law ever pesters you about my whereabouts, later tonight. Let's just say I ain't out to fool around with another gal and I sincerely wish I could fool some more with you. But I can't."

She looked worried as she gasped, "Oh Lord, where are you going so late at night, Frank?"

He replied, "I just tell you that you don't want to know and in any case I ain't certain. Somebody will be meeting me out back at midnight and that's all I can tell you. So don't worry about my not carrying you home after work and don't abuse your pretty little self without saving some for me."

She laughed and said he'd pay for that remark, later. Then she had to get back to fleecing the johns, so he nursed his beer a spell and then went out back to stand in the dark, wishing that fucking cat would just let somebody fuck her and shut up about wanting it so bad. She reminded Longarm of some gals he'd met in his own tomcat days.

He was sure it was after midnight when a familiar shemale voice let loose with, "Mr. Mason? Are you there, Mr. Mason?"

Longarm crunched down the alley to meet little Phoebe Blake as, behind him, another familiar she-male voice wailed, "I knew you were meeting another woman back here, you two-timing bastard!"

"Who's that?" asked the little sparrow in a scared tone.

Longarm led her off into the darkness by one elbow, saying, "Just a gal I used to know. Don't worry about it. I was wondering how I'd ever manage a graceful exit in any case. Where are you taking me, ma'am?"

She said, "To meet the others, across from that bank Bob surely told you about. It's not far. That's why Bob told you to wait for me in back of the Palace."

She proved her reassuring words by leading him less than three city blocks toward the U.P. tracks to where, sure enough, Oregon Bob and a trio of other men were standing in the inky shadows of the overhand in front of a closed and shuttered fodder and seed shop.

As he shook with the cadaverous Lefty Lindwood who Oregon Bob had only introduced as "the boss," Longarm hoped the darkness would blur his own features as well. He tried to pitch his voice a tad higher than usual when he casually asked where the buckboard Bob had mentioned might be.

Lefty said, "Around the other side of the block. I decided it was more prudent not to have it parked in front of yonder bank so late for no good reason. This shorter cuss would be Thumbless Mike, who now knows more about nitro than he used to. He assures us he can peel a vault open without waking up the whole town. I'm waiting to see that, or hear that, before waiting around long enough to load a buckboard."

Then, as a distant clock struck midnight, Lefty added, "Shall we get on with it, gents?"

Longarm asked, "Where do you want me posted, boss?"

Lefty said, "Stick with me. I just told you I've made some changes. If this yegg I've never worked with before fucks up, we'll all want to run in a bunch with our guns drawn!"

Thumbless Mike muttered, "Aw, I guess I know a thing or two about high explosives, boss."

With Lefty in the lead, they broke cover to cross the moonlit, but otherwise dark, street. The street lamps of Ogallala only held enough oil to burn 'til ten or so, since most folk who go to bed with the chickens have no call for street lamps.

Lefty led them up to the front door of the dark, deserted bank. He said, "Do your stuff, Thumbless." And the short yegg only took a tad over a minute, sneering at the Yale lock company.

As Lefty led them all into the dark bank, little Phoebe said she was scared. Lefty said, "Go 'round and wait with Verona and the team, then. Bob and Dinky, draw those window blinds so's we can have some light on the subject."

It only took a few moments to make it pitch black and then they lit up the inside of the bank. Longarm spied the dynamite boxes on the floor in front of the tellers' cages and marveled, "What the hell!" just as Oregon Bob knocked him flat on his face so Thumbless Mike and Dinky Cole could dive on top of him.

It got pretty exciting for a spell as Longarm got pistol-whipped and Dinky Cole wound up with a bloody nose. Then Longarm was tied and gagged, seated upright in some banker's swivel chair to stare in dawning dismay at the alarm clock and dry cell battery atop the middle box of sixty percent Nobel brand dynamite!

"Did you really think I'd forget your fucking face in less than a hundred years, Longarm?" Lefty Lindwood laughed in a surprisingly boyish tone. When Longarm didn't answer because he couldn't, Lefty said, "Let's not argue about it. Even if I've already killed you once, it will be fun to kill you again. And if you're really somebody else, as Bob, here, insists, you'll still be worth more to us dead!"

Like most self-styled master criminals, Lefty Lindwood enjoyed pontificating over his own evil genius, so he sneered, "How's that, you ask? Why would I just as soon blow up an otherwise worthless total stranger who dresses like a clown? Because he has to be either crazy or a lawman trying to look like an asshole. Well, seeing by that dollar alarm clock that we've plenty of time, I'll tell you how things are really fixing to go tonight!"

Stepping over to the timer atop the dynamite, Lefty pointed down to explain, "When we were in here earlier, as I'm sure you've guessed by now, Thumbless rigged this simple but certain timer up to go off at two A.M. and, as you see, it's going on one. So in one hour, I hope it's a long hour for you, you son of a bitch, that one hand left on that clock will touch the paper clip stuck with chewing gum to complete the circuit as you're staring at it, and that will be the last sight you'll ever see because Thumbless assures me you and everything else in this fucking bank will be fluttering down in bits and pieces as the echoes fade away!"

Enjoying himself like hell, Lefty gloated. "But *why*, you ask? I'll *tell* you why, you son of a bitch!"

Striking a pose, Lefty said, "Aside from overdue revenge, this is not the only bank we let ourselves into earlier tonight. That buckboard you mentioned is parked on the far side of this block, across from the other bank we *really* mean to rob! Thumbless here, has already primed their vault with nitro. It awaits but a solid blow with his sledge to open like a sardine can! But as good as he is, our prince of yeggs can hardly hope to blow a safe at two A.M. without enough noise to wake up a lot of folk. So that's where you and all this dynamite come in, Longarm."

Pointing at the ticking alarm clock, Lefty explained, "We have our pocket watches syncronized with this timer. At exactly the same minute you die with one hell of a bang on this street, we'll set off our much smaller charge on the far side of the block."

He laughed at the picture he was painting and said, "*This* blast will more than muffle *our* little pop and bring the whole town running, to the ruins of *this* bank, as we clean out that other bank. Before you try to say there's a chance someone might come down the wrong street as we are making our withdrawal, that's why all of us are wearing guns. Nothing is certain but, as you have to admit, I've shaved the odds a heap and ain't you sorry you didn't have the sense to leave such a clever boy alone?"

Had Longarm been able to speak, he'd have wryly agreed there might have been a few flaws in his own plan. But he could barely manage a muffled attempt that wouldn't come out as "Fuck you!" no matter how hard he tried.

The others had trouble meeting Longarm's eye. Oregon Bob quietly suggested, "It's getting late, Lefty."

The mortal enemy, who felt so good about having Longarm at his mercy, said, "We got plenty of time. Things are all set up. But maybe you're right. Maybe we ought to let this wiseass meditate alone as he gets to watch what's left of his life tick away."

He laughed like a gal being tickled and taunted, "*Tick, tick, tick* and I'll see you in hell, Longarm!"

Then he grumped out ahead of everyone else. Oregon Bob lingered long enough to say, "I hope you understand that if it was up to me, I'd just shoot you, Longarm."

Longarm tried to snort, "You're all heart!" but all that came out was a stiffled sound.

Then he was alone in the otherwise deserted bank, staring at that cheap fucking alarm clock by the light of the one oil lamp they'd left burning, on Lefty Lindwood's orders, so he could do just that!

It sure beat all how fast the hour hand of a clock could move when it was fixing to blow up three boxes of dynamite in your goggle-eyed face!

Longarm wondered if it wouldn't be better to shut his eyes so's he'd never know exactly how long he had until he was dead and could never know anything again. But that wouldn't work. A man staring death in the face could only shut his eyes for a second before he just had to stare some more!

Grasping at straws inside his helpless head, Longarm could only hope a drunk staggering home from some cardhouse or worse might notice a light in the window of a bank that was supposed to be closed for the night and . . . Shit, that was why they'd pulled down all those thick green window shades.

Then he hoped it was possible the clock might stop. Clocks stopped all the time when you forgot to wind them. But not before you set them up to kill a man in less than a fucking hour!

But what if the spring broke or, better yet, he might somehow shake that paper clip loose from clear over here . . . ?

The floor was tiled with marble squares, over wood planking, he hoped. He tried stamping his bound boots on the floor in hopes of getting it to vibrate some.

It didn't want to. He studied the crude but effective timer they'd set up. Thumbless, most likely, had known what he was doing with duck soup simple gear he'd doubtless bought in town that afternoon!

He'd removed the glass and minute hand of the dollar alarm clock. Then he'd grounded one wire attached to the dry cells to the on and off button atop the clock. The bare end of the other wire was twisted around that paper clip, insulated from the brass of the clock by that chewing gum. He knew a dynamite cap he'd never see would go off the second that hour hand and that paper clip completed the circuit and, at the rate that fucking hour hand was racing, he didn't have much time if he meant to get himself out of this fix!

But no matter what he tried, he couldn't make it work. He tried in vain to spit out the gag so he could call out, from inside a fucking building, in hopes of waking up someone inside another fucking building!

He tried rocking in the heavy swivel chair so's he could wind up flat on the floor instead of sitting up, as if that might matter, when he couldn't budge the damned fine knots of the latigo leather thongs they'd tied him with.

He wriggled and jiggled, he twisted and turned, and all he got for his effort was a shirt soaked through with sweat under his thick pea coat, and he could see by the clock on that box of dynamite that he had less than half an hour left.

He swore and muttered under his spit-soaked gag, "Well, shit, Mr. Death. We always knew we had to meet up *some* damn time."

Then he shook his head and said, "Fuck you, Mr. Death! This child ain't ready to go!"

Mr. Death, as such, never answered. He just kept going *tick, tick, tick . . .*

Chapter 19

Longarm had been feeling mightly lonesome until he heard Phoebe Blake complain, "Gee, that was awfully mean of Lefty, even if you are a dead lawman, Mr. Mason!"

He couldn't tell if she'd slipped back in or never left. It didn't matter. He managed enough of a wet muffled reply to inspire her to come around from the back of him and take the gag out of his mouth asking, "Does that feel better? I dasn't untie you. Lefty would kill me. But I could suck you off, if you want."

Longarm dryly croaked, "First stop that clock and then we'll talk! We're running out of time, here, Miss Phoebe!"

The drab little sparrow moved over to the infernal setup uncertain as to how it worked. She said, "I don't know how to shut things off. Maybe if I turned back the clock?"

He warned, "Make sure you turn it *back* then!"

She did, then turned to stare wistfully down at him from her modest height as she said, "I'm awfully sorry about this, Mr. Mason. I know we're on opposite sides but I sure wish we weren't. For you've been one of the few gents who ever made me feel like a lady and I'll really miss you when you're gone!"

Longarm asked, "Why do we have to be on opposite sides, Miss Phoebe? You're still young, with your whole life ahead of you! A better life than you've been leading, if you'd let me show you how to dress and fix your hair! You saw how Oregon Bob left you to fend for yourself down at the depot the other day. You've told me yourself none of them treat you like a lady!"

She sobbed, "They're the only ones I can ride with. It's too late to talk about changing sides. As nice as you've always treated me, it would be your bound duty to turn me in to the hangman if you knew who I really was and you ever had the chance!"

"Tell me who your really are and let me be the judge of that," he suggested in as calm a tone as he could manage.

She hesitated, shrugged in resignation, and decided, "Why not, seeing you can't never tell and it weighs heavy on my mind."

She took a deep breath and declared, as if announcing the Second Coming that her real last name was Boggs.

Longarm smiled up at her uncertainly and replied "I'm sorry to hear that, Miss Phoebe but, no offense, the name ain't famous, neither."

She said, "I killed my very own father, back in Tennessee. I blew his head off with his own scatter gun. I gave him both barrels in the face, and I still ain't sorry, so there!"

Longarm quietly suggested. "I'm sure you had what you thought was a good motive, Miss Phoebe."

She sniffed, "I was sure, too. But when I told Lefty all about it, early on, he said it was too seriously disgusting a killing to fix."

Longarm said, "I know a thing or two about courtroom

proceedings, Miss Phoebe. Why don't you tell me about the killing, your ownself?"

The waifish little thing sniffed and said, "It began when I was an only child of six and we'd just buried my ma up the holler. Pappy had been a hard-drinking man when she was there to nag him. Once she was gone and there was just the two of us in the cabin, Pappy got to drinking more, carrying on with the livestock and asking me to kiss Pappy goodnight, all over."

Longarm whistled and wondered, "He committed incest with a six-year-old daughter?"

She asked, "Is that a fancy word for cocksucking? He made me bleed, trying to treat me like his redbone bitch when she was in heat. He taught me to suck his cock and I confess I really liked it when he licked my little pink slit in return. I knew what we were doing was wrong in the eyes of the church by the time I was old enough for him to fuck me like a woman. But it felt so grand I didn't care and by now I was really in love, womanly love, with the onliest man who'd ever kissed me!"

Longarm soberly said, "I can understand that. Odd as it may sound. Speaking as a lawman, I can tell you such goings on go on more than any church approves. But how come you blew his head off with his own scatter gun if you were all that fond of him, Miss Phoebe?"

She pouted, "He wanted me to fuck and suck another moonshiner for a wagonload of jars! The one and only man I loved, my own Pappy, pimping for me like I was . . . *livestock!*"

Longarm whistled again and said, "Some I know would say a man like your dad don't deserve to live, no offense, and it only takes one such opinion of a jury of twelve to get you off. Have you ever killed anybody else, Miss Phoebe? I have to know before I make you any false promises."

She sniffed, "I've killed nobody but my Pappy. Ain't

171

that enough to hang a girl? What kind of promises might a man about to die make anybody? I didn't want them to kill you, but as you see, they have, and I only wanted to offer you some comfort before you go. Would you like me to suck you off, now? We ain't got much time, Mr. Mason."

He said, "My friends call me Custis, Miss Phoebe. I wouldn't have to die, and you wouldn't have to worry about hanging if you cut me loose and helped me get away."

She sighed and said, "Aw, you're just saying that to pull the wool over my eyes. I may be low-down and dirty, but I ain't stupid! We all know they hang a girl for killing her own Pappy!"

He insisted, "Not one who'd molest his own child and try to turn her into a whore, Miss Phoebe! I've seen a lot of gals gets off after they killed less offensive gents! I'm sure you must have read of that Denver lady who shot a husband she wasn't *kin* to when he offered her favors in exchange for a gambling debt."

Phoebe hadn't. So he tried, "Well, never mind. Let's say I know a Denver judge I can fix for you if you'd cut me loose and run away to Denver with me, Miss Phoebe! I'll take you to Romano's for a genuine Eye-talian supper and show you Pike's Peak from the roof of our federal building. If you want, I'll carry you to this beauty salon run by a pal of mine and gussy you up pretty as anything before we see that judge about getting you off on justifiable homicide."

She sniffed and said, "Well, I don't know. You wouldn't be the first man who fibbed to me just to have his own wicked way!"

He said, "Cut me loose or turn that clock back some more! We are purely running out of time here, girl!"

It might have been the male voice of command. She might have just had more common sense than she'd shown up until them. But she whipped out a bitty pen knife to cut his latigo bonds with a skill that seemed sort of ominous, seeing she'd just said she'd never murdered all that many.

Longarm sprang up, staggered and headed for the door stamping the circulation back in his limbs as somewhere in the distance that same town clock chimed two A.M.

He trimmed the one lamp just inside the entrance and shoved the door open, asking her if she was packing a gun.

She said she had a five shot .32 muff pistol in a garter holster. He took her by one hand and hightailed it across the street to the deep shade on the far side before he asked her for it.

She hoisted her slate gray skirts, her petite legs weren't bad at all, to produce the bitty, nickel-plated and under-powered two-dollar pistol, sniffing, "You'd better not be trifling with me! I guess you know this means I'll never be able to go back to Lefty!"

He said, "Screw Lefty!" and she giggled, "I already have!" as he whipped them both into a slot through the block to put some distance between them and five seriously armed killers until he could get his hands on a serious gun!

While all this had been going on, Lefty and the others in another nearby bank had stared at one another bemused when that distant clock struck two and they didn't hear another sound as they waited, and then waited some more.

Lefty glared at Thumbless Mike, as puzzled as anyone, standing there with that sledge in his hands and a blank look on his face.

Lefty said, "You told me you knew how to set up the infernal machine. I don't hear no infernal machine going off right now. How did you fuck up this time, you fumble-fingered fuck-up?"

Thumbless Mike defensively replied, "How the fuck

173

should I know? I set things to go off at two! Unless *you* fucked up with those knots, it has to be a short circuit or mebbe dead dry cells. I wasn't the one as bought them dry cells, neither!"

Drawing his six-gun, Lefty said, "Let's go back and have a look. We ain't got all night!"

As he led Thumbless Mike and Dinky Cole to the alley entrance they had forced open, Oregon Bob yelled, "Hold on, Lefty! I can think of a worse disaster than a dead dry cell!"

But Lefty Lindwood had been insisting all along he was smarter than anyboy riding on either side of the law. So as the three of them vanished, Oregon Bob muttered, "Aw, shit!" and popped the sprung front door from the inside, as they had the other, to dash out and across that street to where Verona O'Shay was holding the buckboard team.

As Oregon Bob joined her, Verona asked what was up. He grabbed on to her and said, "Tell you along the way. Things are headed for hell in a hack, and we got to get your pretty little ass out of here!"

As he half led and half hauled her down the dark, deserted street, the Junoesque Verona warned, "Watch your manners. I'm Lefty's private pussy, Bob!"

Then the ground shifted under them, window glass shattered all around, and a mighty blast of three boxes of sixty percent Nobel was heard clear out to the D Bar D when it all went off in the face of Lefty and his fellow killers, wiping their faces and all the rest of the meat from their shattered bones.

Over on the far side of the blast, Longarm and Phoebe ran into Jeb Folsom and two other night deputies tearing towards the source of all that noise with their guns drawn.

Deputy Folsom said, "Stop right there, Frank Mason, and account for your being out on the street at this hour amid all these echoes!"

Longarm said, "I ain't Frank Mason. I'm Deputy U.S. Marshal Custis Long and this lady is a federal material witness!"

Folsom gasped, "Jesus H. Christ! Are you trying to say you're the famous Longarm they already killed?"

Longarm said, "That was the first mistake they made. You just now heard another. If you'd care to be famous, too, get me a six-gun and give me a hand lest any survivors get away!"

Jeb Folsom yelled at his own nearest follower, "You heard the man! Give him your six-gun and escort this lady over to the office!"

As Phoebe wailed she'd been betrayed, Longarm assured her, "You just heard me say you were a material witness, not a prisoner, and it's gonna be all right. You'll see."

Then he accepted the cheap but reliable Colt single action he'd been offered, with a nod of thanks, and added, "*Vamanos, muchachos*, over to the municipal corral!"

As Folsom and the other Keith County lawman kept pace with him, they naturally wanted to know why. Longarm grunted, "Where else might you be headed at this hour, with neither trains nor stage coaches leaving this side of dawn, if you felt you had to get out of town in a hell of a hurry?"

So they hurried on to the municipal corral and when Longarm spied a familiar male figure and a gal in a riding habit jawing with a colored stable hand in the lamplit dooway of the livery office, Longarm slid to a walk and cautioned, "Spread out, pussyfoot, and let me see if I can take him alive."

But Oregon Bob, having ridden the owlhoot trail on edge for a spell, spotted Longarm coming and whirled away from the she-male prize he'd just claimed to grab for his own side arm!

175

Longarm yelled, "Don't make me do it! I got the drop on you, Bob!"

But Oregon Bob slapped leather with the reckless smile of a man with nothing to lose. So Longarm did what he had to do, with his horse pistol trained on the desperate killer, and Oregon Bob wound up flat on his back in the dust with his she-male companion screaming like a banshee about how cruel Longarm was.

Longarm let Keith County deal with the pesky gal as he walked on to where Oregon Bob lay, hunkered down, and said, "Evening, Bob. As you see, I ain't dead after all. Were you and that lady the only ones who escaped that blast meant for me?"

Oregon Bob tried to smile up into the lamplight gallantly. But it got tough to look gallant when bloody foam kept bubbling out of your smile.

Longarm said, "Never mind. I can see you don't want to discuss any offers of immunity, now, and we can sort it all out by counting the boots scattered amid the ruins. Good riding boots, or at least their heels, can make it through most anything."

Oregon Bob didn't answer. He wasn't even blowing bubbles, now.

As Longarm rose back to his considerable height, he was joined over the body by Deputy Folsom, who said, "That lady who was calling you a fiend from hell says she wants to turn state's evidence now."

Longarm strode over to where the distraught Verona was sobbing with her head buried in the vest of another lawman. He had no hat brim to tick to her. So he just said, "Your servant, ma'am. To save us both a heap of time, I doubt there's a thing you can tell us about the late Lefty Lindwood and company that we don't already know, save for the one little secret that could see you off free and clear if you'd care to cooperate with the only friend you have in the world right now."

Verona turned from the county law to throw herself in Longarm's arms as she sobbed, "Anything! I'll do anything you ask, for I'm too young and pretty to go to prison!"

He patted her back, brothersome, and said, "A judge I know who can let most anyone off or hang 'em high will be grateful as all get-out if you can name that political fixer who got Lefty Lindwood out when he was supposed to be serving life at hard."

But Verona O'Shay swore she didn't know and, considering the time at hard she was facing, it seemed likely she really didn't know, so she really had been beautiful but dumb and *now* what in thunder was the lawman after that fixer supposed to do about such a total dead end?

Chapter 20

Most everybody within sound of the mighty blast was up for the night but it was well after daybreak by the time they got things sorted out.

The bank the gang had tried to rob was in far better shape than the one they tried to blow up. But neither safe had been cracked and everyone's savings were safe. The three charred and widely scattered pair of boots and the two women questioned separately confirmed that all the male members of the gang were dead. They recovered Longarm's .44-40 and double derringer along with Thumbless Mike's safe cracking gear in the undamaged bank.

Verona O'Shay was being held in the county jail so's various courts from all over creation could bid on her extradition. Longarm checked the drab little Phoebe Blake, or Boggs, into the room Salome Morrigan had stayed in at the Ogallala Overland Rest while he awaited answers to some wires.

Meanwhile, he bought himself some sensible duds as he retired the flashy Frank Mason, seeing everybody knew who he really was. It was safe to eat in that Tex-Mex chili parlor across the way now, and seeing Phoebe had shown a liking for *chili verde con carne* earlier, he took her to lunch there.

As they et whilst the waitress who loved him pouted, Longarm told the ragged looking waif, "I got time to run you over to a notions shop and buy you a more decent outfit, Miss Phoebe. But I fear I may have to leave you alone at the hotel for the rest of the day. I promised a newspaper pal an exclusive interview and it's likely to take me some time."

She asked if he was sure about that pardon for killing her pappy.

He soothed, "Duck soup simple. Your degenerate dad had it coming, and you saved the life of a federal lawman and helped him crack a way more serious case."

Then he sighed and added, "Almost, least ways. The more serious crook my court was after seems to have got away, since dead men tell no tails. But I promised you I'd fix any charges against you and I'm a man of my word."

She sighed and said, "I surely hope so. But are you sure you can afford it? Lefty told me he couldn't spare the retail for his big shot lawyer in Leavenworth to fix my case until after we robbed some more banks."

Longarm nodded absently and signaled the sullen waitress for more coffee to go with the fiery grub they were having. Then he shot a sharp look at Phoebe to ask, "He talked to you about a big shot lawyer down in Leavenworth, Miss Phoebe? He told you how much this jasper asked as a *retainer* before he put in the fix?"

She said, "Sure, Lefty liked to talk in bed, afterwards, like any other natural man. He said the big shot lawyer was a squire by the name of Bastard . . . Naw, that ain't it . . . Bascomb! That was what Lefty called the bastard. It was Lefty said he was a bastard. I never met his lawyer in Leavenworth."

Longarm said, "I feel certain Lefty knew what he was

180

talking about. Finish your grub and let's get you on back to the hotel, Miss Phoebe. I see I got more telegrams to send."

After he'd seen her safely back to the hotel and before he went to be interviewed in the depths of Tess Coletti that afternoon, Longarm got off wires to the Leavenworth bar associate for a list of lawyers named Bascomb and a sneakier one to a Denver pal on the nationwide political committee of the Grand Old Party.

Whilst he was at it, he sent wires to pals in the know with both the Democrats and Grange movement. He didn't see how a Socialist or the Fenians could fix a federal life sentence.

Then there was nothing to do but wait and wait some more as he had his fill of *menudo* with Phoebe and minestrone with Tess. Two-timing so tight would have been unwise had Phoebe appealed to him. So by the time he had everything set up for his next move, he suspected good old Tess might be hankering for a change, as well.

Just before he was ready to take Phoebe down to Leavenworth in the new fall outfit he'd bought her with his expense account, seeing she was a federal witness in disguise, Longarm got an engraved invitation on high-toned paper to the engagement party of Una Clarke née MacAlpin and, for Pete's sake, Duke Roberts.

Leavenworth, Kansas, a short riverboat ride up the Big Muddy from Kansas City, was where they'd built the Jefferson Barracks they'd converted into a military and federal prison as the frontier moved further west.

When they got there, Longarm hired them adjoining rooms in a hotel near the prison. By then, he'd learned by wire that the Lawyer Bascomb, said to fix things better than Boss Tweed, was an Aaron Burr Bascomb with a fancy office down in Kansas City.

Because Phoebe had to have an excuse to meet with him in her Leavenworth hotel, instead of his K.C. office, she sent the lawyer a handwritten note, which Longarm dictated, saying she was anxious about a someone she declined to name, locked up in Jefferson Barracks over a silly misunderstanding.

The fifty-dollar retainer sent along with the letter was better than a top hand's monthly wages, and Longarm had had a time getting Billy Vail to go along with the gesture.

The fixer he was out to fix didn't snap at the bait right off, of course. That was why he'd brought Lefty Lindwood's known love slave along. Kansas was one of the few dry states. So they had to go out to eat and drink three times a day at establishments where you weren't supposed to see a lawman. Longarm felt certain Billy would agree, once he studied on it, state dry laws were no never mind of a federal deputy.

The point of all his locally unlawful wining and dining of a lady of low repute along the owlhoot trail was to assure the sneaks that Lawyer Bascomb was sure to send up the river ahead of him that the lady in such need of his legal advice was no lady. Longarm had changed into yet another tinhorn outfit, lest they think Lefty's doxie had sunk to ordering her own drinks without an escort!

It took seventy-two hours of such sniffing before they got word the lawyer was on his way. Longarm knew he'd have never bit had both of them been total strangers who just *looked* disreputable.

They put Phoebe in a red velvet gown to greet the portly lawyer of, say, fifty, who showed up with a "secretary" young enough to get his *son* nailed on statutory, if he hadn't been such a fixer.

Phoebe and her two guests set whilst Longarm, as *her* backup, built a round of illegal drinks at the sideboard, banging and clanging the jars until Lawyer Bascomb said, "Would you mind, Mr. Short? We're trying to get a handle on this little lady's problem, here."

So, knowing the fixer had read the newspaper accounts

of a former client's death by dynamite, Phoebe gave the name of a bank robber in the nearby prison, who would have been surprised to hear a gal he had never met was so much in love with him. She told Lawyer Bascomb the law had no idea the man doing five on a lesser charge had been in on a killing with Lefty and the boys.

She explained, "You might have heard they're holding Verona O'Shay and sweating her about all that noise up Ogallala way. If she talks, and I fear she will to save her own neck, poor Vincent, over to those Jefferson Barracks, is sure to be charged with a killing he never meant. Him and Lefty had agreed to go easy on the bank staff but how were they to know this teller gal would pull a gun on them?"

Lawyer Bascomb and his bitty brunette exchanged thoughtful glances. Then, as Longarm handed out the drinks, Bascomb warned, "Shooting any women is a bother to fix, Miss Phoebe. Shooting a brave woman defending the money of her bank's depositors is going to be, sorry, ladies, a real bitch!"

"We heard you can get anybody off, on any charge," said Longarm in as admiring a tone as he could manage, adding, "You must be some lawyer, Lawyer Bascomb!"

Bascomb shrugged modestly and said, "Miss Phoebe's Vincent will be defended in court by a younger associate, aided by Miss Alfrieda, here."

Longarm nodded at Phoebe, who said, "Are you sure they'll be able to get poor Vincent off?"

Bascomb said, "Not unless we make it worth the while of the judge and at least one juror, Miss Phoebe. There's no way even a lawyer like me could get a bank robber off for the murder of a woman during the commission of a crime if they were to hold a *fair trial*!"

Longarm went back to the sideboard as if to freshen his drink as he laughed, "Are you saying it's that easy to fix a hanging offense?"

Bascomb shrugged and said, "It's never failed me, so far, as long as the client has the money for me to work with. I've got my in with the national party and the judges know which side of their bread I can smear the butter on. The gentlemen of the jury don't run for their own positions. But with twelve of the simps to work with, you can always find one for a price."

Longarm winked at Phoebe and said, "Lefty was right. He said Lawyer Bascomb got him out of life at hard with time served and he was *way* meaner than old Vince."

Turning to Bascomb he asked, "How much did Lefty pay you for that fix, seeing it's about time to get down to what all this is likely to cost us."

Bascomb said, "Two thousand for me and a thousand for the judge who issued the writ. But that was an easier case. Lefty Lindwood was doing time for killing a man! So it's time indeed to get down to brass tacks about my fee and expenses!"

Longarm said, "No need to bother, Lawyer Bascomb. I've heard enough. My name ain't really Cassius Clay Short. I'm Deputy U.S. Marshal Custis Long and you two are under arrest now."

The bitty Alfrieda gleeped, "Oh, no! I warned you we didn't know these people, Aaron!"

The older man said, "Tush, that's why I brought you along, my dear. It's my word with you as my witness against a woman of low repute and a clumsy attempt at entrapment by a tin star who should brush up on his rules of evidence!"

Longarm said, "I have," and banged the sideboard three times with the bottom of a whiskey jar.

Whereupon the sliding doors to the adjoining room slid open to admit three more men and a chestnut-headed gal with a note pad in her hands.

Longarm explained to the startled fixer and his one witness, "This tall, hatchet-faced cuss would be Deputy Smiley of the Denver District Court. The shorter one dressed cow would be Deputy Dutch. The fatter cuss in the checked suit and derby would be Reporter Crawford of the *Denver Post*. This pretty little thing smiling at you so mean would be Reporter Coletti of the *Omaha Herald* and other papers across this land. I promised the both of them exclusives when this case was over and as you see, it's over. I sent for Smiley and Dutch to take you in. I got other rows to hoe before I head back for Denver, myself."

Alfrieda was starting to bawl. She figured to turn state's evidence. Bascomb sneered, "I'll be out on a writ before you can file your foolish report!"

Longarm shrugged and said, "That well may be. On the other hand, how many friends in the national committee do you reckon you'll have after all this hits the newspapers nationwide?"

"I want a lawyer! Not *this* asshole!" wailed Alfrieda.

So as things turned out, Judge Dickerson was saved the bother of prosecuting a Kansas fixer in Colorado because a whole raft of Kansas judges fought over who got to try such a crooked politician to prove *they* weren't crooked politicians.

For it was an election year and as Longarm had predicted, old Aaron Burr Bascomb didn't have a political pull in the world after both Tess Coletti and Reporter Crawford filed separate but confirming versions of the arrest.

The *Kansas City Star* was so impressed with the chubby little gal's big news-wire scoop, they offered Tess a staff job just down the river. Longarm assured Tess he understood why she had to light out on him so suddenly after blowing taps for the last time on his French horn.

Longarm never asked Phoebe Boggs to kiss him goodbye above or below the belt buckle. Nor did he ask her where she was headed.

As he'd promised Phoebe, a letter from his home office

to the governor of Tennessee got those old charges dropped. For anyone could see a gal who might murder a pimping pappy but saved the life of a famous lawman couldn't be all bad.

Hence Longarm's conscience was clear when he got back to Denver a week or three after Smiley and Dutch. But Billy Vail called him back to his oak-paneled inner office anyway to snap, "Don't you dare light one of them cheroots to discourage my carpet mites and stand up straight whilst you tell me where in blue blazes you've *been* all this time! The crooks we sent you after have been dead or incarcerated for a coon's age!"

Longarm explained, "Promised the sheriff of Keith County I'd drop by on my way home and help him conclude our investigation in this here election year. That's what you call it when you give speeches at local teas or Grange halls, concluding an investigation. After that I had to stand as best man for another pal over yonder. Duke Roberts could have been a total pain in the ass, but he wasn't, so I owed him."

Billy Vail grumped, "Well, all right then. But it's lucky for you that reporter gal who was so much help to you never went back to Ogallala with you. You didn't think I knew about her, did you?"

Longarm just grinned sheepishly, glad old Billy hadn't found out about the chili parlor across from the Ogallala Overland Rest. Or how, seeing he hadn't been dead certain which of those Tex-Mex gals had said she loved him, he'd wound up with *both* of them saying they loved him, up in Room 2-F.

Watch for

LONGARM AND THE POISONERS

293rd novel in the exciting LONGARM series
from Jove

Coming in April!

Explore the exciting Old West with one of the men who made it wild!